T. F. Young

Canada and Other Poems

T. F. Young

Canada and Other Poems

ISBN/EAN: 9783744711951

Printed in Europe, USA, Canada, Australia, Japan

Cover: Foto ©Andreas Hilbeck / pixelio.de

More available books at **www.hansebooks.com**

AND OTHER POEMS.

BY

T. F. YOUNG.

𝔗𝔬𝔯𝔬𝔫𝔱𝔬:

HUNTER, ROSE & CO., PRINTERS.

1887.

PREFACE.

I INTRODUCE the following poetical attempts to the public, with great diffidence. I am not sure but a direct apology would be in better taste, but the strength derived from the purpose I had in view, in writing and publishing them, sustains me without saying anything further by way of excuse. Like Burns, I wished to do something for my country, and chose this method of doing it.

The literature of this country is in its infancy. It must not always remain so, or the expectations we have in regard to making it a great nation, will never be fulfilled. Literature gives life to a nation, or rather it is the reflection of a nation's life and thought, in a mirror, which cheers, strengthens and ennobles those who look into it, and study what is there displayed. Literature must grow with our nation, and, when growing, it will aid the latter's progress in no small degree.

Pedantic critics may find fault with my modest productions, and perhaps justly, in regard to grammatical construction, and mechanical arrangement, but I shall be satisfied, if the public discern a vein of true poetry glittering here and there through what I have just written. The public are the final judges of compositions of this sort, and not the writer himself, or his personal friends. It is they, therefore, who must decide whether these humble attempts of my 'prentice hand, shall be numbered with writings that have been forgotten, or whether their author shall be encouraged to strike his lyre in a higher key, to accompany his Muse, while she tries to sing in a loftier strain.

In passing an opinion on my literary venture, of course the youthful state of our country will be taken into consideration, for it is a state which necessarily tinges all of our productions, literary or otherwise, with a certain amount of crudity. Consequently, reasonable men will not expect that felicity of expression, and that ripeness and happiness of thought, which would be expected in the productions of an older country, although they may be aware that true poetry is not the result of education, or even the refinements of a nation long civilized.

With these words by way of introduction and explanation, I dedicate this little book of mine to the Canadian public, hoping that whatever they may think of me as a poet, they will not forget that I am a loyal Canadian, zealous in behalf of anything that may tend to refine, instruct and elevate my country, and anxious to see her take an honorable stand among the other nations of the earth.

THE AUTHOR.

PORT ALBERT, March, 1887.

CONTENTS.

----◆----

CONTENTS.

POEMS.

NEW YEAR'S DAY.

HAIL! joyous morn. Hail! happy day,
That ushers in another year,
Fraught with what sorrow, none can say,
Nor with what pain, to mortals here.

Another year has roll'd away,
With all its sorrows, joys and fears,
But still the light of hope's glad ray,
Yet beams within our heart, and cheers.

One year, one span of time has pass'd,
So swift to some, to others slow;
But it has gone, and we should cast
Along with it, remorse and woe.

Of things we've done, or only thought,
'Tis useless now the bitter tear,
Of actions unavailing wrought,
Let them repose upon their bier.

We should, indeed, e'en yet atone
For what our reason says we can,
But never let remorse's groan
Degrade us from our state as man.

Let us discharge the debts we owe,
But still some debts will be unpaid;
But we, if we forgive, also,
Should ne'er, despairing, feel afraid.

The future is before us still,
And to that future we should gaze,
With hope renew'd, with firmer will,
To tread life's weary, tangl'd maze.

We ne'er should let the gloomy past,
Bow down our heads in dark despair,
But we should keep those lessons fast,
Which e'en our follies taught us there.

Experience, so dearly bought,
By folly, or by ignorance,
Should, in our inmost system wrought,
Our daily life improve, advance.

Then let us press towards the goal,
The common goal of all mankind,
Go on, while seasons onward roll,
Nor cast one fainting look behind.

And, as we journey through this year,
Let us in watchfulness beware
Of all that brings remorseful tear,
Or future terror and despair.

Let us with thoughtful vision scan
Each step we take, each act we do,
That we may meet our brother man,
With no unrighteous thing to rue.

A happy, happy, bright New Year,
I wish to all the sons of men,
With happy hearts, and merry cheer,
Till it has roll'd its round again.

TO A CANARY.

Imprison'd songster, thou for me
Hath warbl'd many a cheerful lay,
Thy songs, so sweetly glad and free,
Revive my heart, from day to day.

The frost is keen, the wind is cold,
No wild-bird twitters from the spray,
But, still resounding as of old,
Thy voice thrills forth, and seems to say:

"Wake up ! O sadden'd mortal, wake !
Shake off that anxious, careworn frown,
Thy hopes renew, fresh courage take,
Nor let your troubles weigh you down.

"See, I am happy all alone,
And, kept behind the prison bars,
I sing, and shouldst thou ever moan ?
—A mortal free, beneath the stars.

"I fly around my narrow cage,
I sing the song that gladdens you,
But carking care thy thoughts engage,
While walking free, 'neath heaven's blue.

"My heart might faint, my spirit die,
Far from my kind, and from my home,
But cheerfully I sing and fly,
Beneath my narrow prison's dome.

"Oh, list, sad mortal to my song,
And, while thou hearest, mark it well,
And go thy cheerful way along,
Nor pray to know, what none can tell.

"I'll sing my song each day for thee,
And live the moments as they fly,
With gladden'd heart, with sounding glee,
And thou shouldst do the same as I."

AUTOGRAPHS.

TO A LITTLE GIRL.

E ACH wish, my fairest child, I pen,
F or thee I write with earnest heart;
F or who shall say, that ere, again,
I shall behold thee; when we part
E 'en now the time is near, I start.

H ere are my wishes, then, sweet child,
A long life's pathway may thou go,
R ob'd white, as now, in virtue mild,
R etaining pure, thy virtue's snow.
I wish thee this, and wish thee more,—
S o long as thou on earth hath life,
O h! may thy heart be never sore,
N or vex'd with anxious care or strife!

TO A YOUNG LADY.

Short is the time, my friend, since I
First heard thy voice, first saw thy face,
And yet, the days in gliding by,
Have left within my mind a trace—
A friendly trace of thee and thine,
Which I am sure will long remain
Within my heart, to cheer and shine
With other joys, to lessen pain.

It is my hope, also, that thou
May, in thy heart, and on thy tongue,
Have thoughts and words for him, who now
Is yours so friendly, T. F. Young.

KELVIN.

WHILE poets sing in lofty strain,
   And ask where Rome and Carthage are,
This humble village on the plain,
   To many hearts is dearer far.

Then to these hearts I'll sing my lay,
   With humble Kelvin for my theme ;
My song shall be of life to-day,
   And not a retrospective dream.

Of " Kelvin's Grove," some love-lorn swain
   Sang sweetly, many years ago,
And I shall sound the name again,
   Although I may not sound it so.

Of Kelvin's bonnie lasses, I
   Can sing, tho' not so well as he,
And Kelvin's groves, in passing by,
   I can repeat, have charms for me.

And Kelvin's stream, where fishes glide,
   And timid fowl their plumage lave,
Where drooping willows by its side,
   Their graceful branches gently wave.

Here happiness and plenty reign,
   And e'en refinement, too, is seen.
For music sends its cheering strain,
   Where flowers grow within the green.

Here virtuous dames with busy hand,
  Untiring do what should be done,
And sons and fathers till the land,
  And to each manly duty run.

The winsome maids with willing hearts,
  In youthful beauty all aglow,
Right cheerfully perform their parts
  Where duty's voice may bid them go.

Oh, may their graceful figures long
  Their youthful energy retain,
And may they meet no heartless wrong,
  To fill their gentle souls with pain.

As yet there is no village bell,
  Save that which rings the call to school,
Where festive youth drink at the well
  Which flows from knowldge' sparkling pool.

And yet, whene'er the Sabbath comes,
  Or week night held for praise and prayer,
No need for signal bells and drums,
  Each knows the time, and he is there.

There is the daughter, there the son,
  To kneel in humble prayer to God,
And those whose race is well-nigh run,
  Who humbly kiss the chast'ning rod.

Oh, blest content, and lowly life
  That blunts Ambition's biting sting,
Unknown to thee the bitter strife,
  Which proud refinements often bring.

IS THERE ROOM FOR THE POET ?

Is there room for the poet, fair Canada's sons,
To live his strange life, and to warble his songs,
To follow each current of thought as it runs,
And to sing of your victories, glories and wrongs ?

Is there room for the poet, ye senators grave ?
Ye orators, statesmen and law-makers, say;
May he of the calling so gentle e'er crave
Your patronage, and of your kindness a ray ?

Ye toilers in cities, ye workers in fields,
Who handle the hammer, the pen or the plow,
Can the poet implicitly trust, as he yields
His heart, and his hopes, and his name to you now ?

Wilt thou pardon his follies, forgive him his faults
In manners, in habits, in distance and time ?
For when on his charger, Pegasus, he vaults,
He rises o'er reason's safe, temperate clime.

He will sing of his country, his people and thine,
Exalt, if you aid him, your honor and fame.
Your smpathy, acting like purest of wine,
Will urge him to joyously sing of your name.

His case is peculiar, stern fate has been hard,
His body unfitted for labours of men,
His mind, with the sensitive make of the bard,
Unfitted for aught, but the work of the pen. ·

He singeth, but yet he must live, as he sings;
He hath wants of the earth, that must be supplied;
And tho' 'tis an off'ring most humble he brings,
He hopes that your favors will not be denied.

Our country is young, let us early instil
Deep into the minds of the youthful and fair,
The greatness of virtue, uprightness and will,
And the poet will help you to 'stablish them there.

Be it his to proclaim, e'en tho' rudely, in measure,
The rights of his country, her honour, renown ;
To sing of whatever his people may treasure,
In court or in camp, in the country or town.

MAN AND HIS PLEASURES.

'Tis not with glad fruition crown'd,
We always feel our greatest joy ;
For pleasure often dwells around
The heart that hopes, and knows no cloy.

We wait, we watch, we think, we plan
To catch the pleasure ere it flies,
But when 'tis caught, for which we ran,
It often droops, perchance, it dies.

In truth the non-possession oft'
Creates the chief, the only charm,
Of that, which, once obtain'd, is scoft'd,
And oft' receiv'd with vex'd alarm.

The mind of man is strange and deep,
Deceiving others and himself ;
Its wiles would make an angel weep,
In strife for praise, for power and pelf.

Strange mixture of the good and ill,
He strives continually to bend
Those qualities, with wondrous skill,
To meet in one, which never blend.

DAVID'S LAMENTATION OVER SAUL AND JONATHAN.

THE beauty of Isreal is slain on thy mountains,
The mighty are low, and how great is their fall,
But tell not our grief in Gath, by the fountains,
And publish it not within Askelon's wall,
Lest the Philistines' daughters shall mock at our sorrow,
And triumph in gladness o'er us in our pain,
And sound all their timbrels and harps on the morrow,
While here we are sore, in lamenting our slain.

Oh ! Gilboa's mountains, from now and forever,
Let moisture, which falleth as rain, or as dew,
Come down on thy parch'd, burning summits, oh, never,
For the shield of the mighty is cast upon you.
From the blood of the slain, from the fat of the highest,
The bow of fair Jonathan never did quail,
And the sword of his father, in danger the nighest,
Went forth to brave deeds, like the sweep of the gale.

O Saul, thou anointed ! and Jonathan, brother !
In life ye were pleasant and lovely to see ;
And still in your death ye are lovely together,
Tho' great is my grief, and my sorrow, for thee.
Ye were swifter than eagles, ye heaven-anointed,
And stronger than lions, thou glorious pair,
But sad was the day, that Jehovah appointed,
To humble your strength, and your bravery, there.

Oh, weep o'er the fallen, fair Isreal's danghters !
He cloth'd you in scarlet, and deck'd you with gold,
Then shed ye your tears, until their sad waters
Shall moisten the tomb, where now he is cold ;
I'm sad for thee, Jonathan, more than my brother,
So kindly and gentle, so faithful and free,
I lov'd thee, as never I shall love another,
And thou hadst a wonderful love unto me.

The mighty have fallen, their weapons have perish'd !
And, slain in high places, so low lies the brave ;
No more I shall gaze on the face that I cherish'd,
O Jonathan, brother, now cold in thy grave.

THE DIAMOND AND THE PEBBLE.

WHY value ye the diamond, and
The pearl from Ceylon's balmy shore,
When stones unnumber'd strew the land,
And in the sea are millions more ?
Why treasure ye each silver bar,
And watch, with Argus eye, your gold,
When lead and iron, near and far,
Are strewn beneath the rocks and mould.

Ye prize those shining gems, because
Their sparkling beauty cheers the eye,
And, by the force of nature's laws,
They never in profusion lie.
Could we, Aladdin like, descend
Into a place where diamonds grow,
Our minds would then most surely tend
To value diamonds very low.

The emerald's or diamond's shine,
Is valued not for that alone,
But for its absence in the mine,
Where thousands lie, of common stone.
And thus, within the world of thought,
The pebble and the lead abound,
But real pearls are seldom brought,
And gold or silver rarely found.

We all have thoughts, we speak them, too,
The world is fill'd with words of men,

But still is priz'd the precious hue,
Of golden thoughts from tongue or pen ;
And he who digs and brings to light
A lovely thought, a pearly gem,
'Twill surely shine with lustre bright,
For men, to cheer and better them.

———

TEMPTATION.

The greatest glory consists, not in never falling, but in getting up
every time you fall.—CONFUCIUS.

THE raging force of passion's storm,
   Say who can check at will.
Or cope with sin, in ev'ry form,
   With ever conquering skill ?

How oft we've tried, and hop'd and pray'd
   To conquer in the right ;
But still, how oft our hearts, dismay'd,
   Have fail'd amid the fight.

But still we fought the wrong we loath'd,
   And though we fought in vain,
Our wills in fleshly weakness cloth'd,
   Would try the fight again.

And He, I apprehend, who sees,
   And knows our struggles here.
Will lead us onward, by degrees,
   To triumph, though we fear.

And even tho' we're never quit
   Of these sharp earthly thorns,
In black despair we'll never sit,
   Till danger's signal warns.

We'll gird ourselves anew, to fight
    Our fell, determin'd foe,
And with experience's light,
    Each time more skilful grow.

SLANDER.

Of all the poison plants that grow,
And flourish in the human breast,
No other plant, perhaps, hath so
Deep clench'd a root, or peaceful rest.

No other plant has such a fruit,
At once so sweet, and deadly too,
As that which loads each branch and shoot,
And falls for me to eat, and you.

Fell jealousy, the monster wild,
Whose green eyes roll in frenzy round,
His ravages are small, and mild,
To thine, and narrow'r far his ground.

His pow'r is felt around his home,
But who can gauge the sway of thine,
Which reaches high to heaven's dome,
And acts within the darksome mine ?

Thy poison drops distil each hour,
To blight, to ruin and destroy,
And find with dark, insidious pow'r,
The heart of woman, man and boy.

What antidote can neutralize
Thy baneful force, thy potent spell ?
For deepest danger ever lies
Within this poison draught of hell.

And men will drink with eager lip,
The cup thou holdest forth to them,
Not knowing that the draught they sip
May their, and other souls, condemn.

WOMAN.

I'VE had my share of bright employ,
    My share of pain and blame,
But thro' it all, I've thought, with joy,
    Of tender woman's name.

Her healing tones have often brought
    New gladness to my soul;
Her breath hath rent the darken'd clouds,
    That often o'er it roll.

Her voice hath often cheer'd my heart,
    In sickness and in pain,
And help'd me bear the surgeon's knife,
    Or fever's fervid reign.

But, oh, that voice can change its tone,
    That tender feeling die,
Those gentle, loving tones become
    A terrorizing cry.

In kindly sound, a woman's voice
    Is happiness alone ;
And may it ever be my lot
    To hear its tender tone.

But let me never know the thoughts
    Of vengeful woman's heart,
Or hear the voice that breathes them forth,
    With cold and cruel dart.

O woman, thou hast mighty pow'r
　Among the sons of men,
For thou canst make deep, rankling wounds,
　And heal them up again.

Oh, let thy angel nature shine,
　And may we all refrain
To wake the tiger in thy breast,
　Bound by a slender chain.

———

SYMPATHY.

'MID forces all, that work unseen,
　And cheer or warm the human breast,
Thou, Sympathy, hath ever been,
　In active power, amid the rest.
When raging hate, or heedless love,
　Aspir'd to rule and reign alone,
Thou still did keep thy place above,
　And rul'd serenely, from thy throne.

Thou ever dost assert thy right,
　And walkest on thy gentle way,
To rule with mild, persuasive might,
　But with a strong, unconcious sway,
What pow'r thou hast o'er human hearts
　We daily feel, we daily see ;
For men and women act their parts,
　Encourag'd and upheld by thee.

For, in an unseen current runs,
　From heart to heart, from soul to soul,
Thy force, like heat from genial suns,
　To permeate and warm the whole.

Not always, tho', to warm and cheer.
   At times thy influence is chill,
And checks the noble rage of thought,
   As ice can check a flowing rill.

One cutting word of ours can wilt,
   Or blast the young heart's fairest flow'r,
And tumble down air castles built,
   By this unseen affection's pow'r.
That man is brave, who acts his part,
   'Mid comrades faithful, known and brave,
But braver far is he, whose heart
   Upholds itself upon the wave.

For men have shrunk with coward fright,
   At terrors which they ne'er might feel,
Had Sympathy's strange, magic might
   Inspir'd their hearts to face the steel.

LOVE AND WINE.

'TIS wine that cheers the soul of man,
   With subtle and seductive flow ;
It warms the heart, as naught else can,
   And banishes regret, and woe.

It keeps alive the flick'ring flame,
   Which strives to burn with feeble force
Within the heart, so dull and tame,
   But still of life, the present source.

It warms up this fount of life,
   And sends life's fluid here and there ;
And nerves and brain, in gladsome strife,
   Forget their dull and dark despair.

And what is love, if 'tis not wine,
　　Refin'd, distill'd from grossness, tho',
More potent than the juice of vine,
　　And bringing greater joy, and woe ?

Does it not, too, refresh, revive,
　　And oft intoxicate the brain,
And make the being all alive
　　With keenest joy, or keenest pain ?

And does it not when much indulg'd,
　　Or held by slack and yielding hand,
Lead on to woes oft undivulg'd,
　　To crimes unknown, throughout the land ?

Oh ! blessed woman, fruitful vine,
　　Inspiring and enchanting twain,
I pray that neither love nor wine,
　　May o'er my will, resistless reign.

They tell us, that the safest way
　　To 'scape from wine or woman's thrall,
Is to go on from day to day,
　　And never drink, or love, at all.

I could give up the cheering wine,
　　And never taste the siren cup,
But oh, thou woman, nymph divine,
　　I can not, will not give thee up.

———— ——

HOW NATURE'S BEAUTIES SHOULD BE VIEWED.

Should man, with microscopic eye,
View the details of Nature's plan,
Into each nook and corner pry,
And needlessly the hidden scan ?

Should he inspect each bud and flow'r,
With close, unmeant, uncall'd-for look,
And, by his analytic pow'r,
Dissolve each charm of vale or brook?

Should he resolve the rainbow's hues,
Into their prime and simple forms,
And thus the charm dispel, unloose,
Which gladdens us, amid the storms?

Should he, with keen, inquiring look,
Insist on knowing, seeing all,
Which nature made a sealéd book
On this, our strange, terrestrial ball,

'Tis hard to draw the line, indeed,
When we should pry, and when refrain,
But science surely has its meed
Of knowledge gain'd, and also pain.

The blooming flow'r, the flutt'ring leaf,
Have surely charms we all can tell,
And analysing brings to grief,
The charms we felt, and knew so well.

Th' untutor'd savage, roaming wild,
Could view the rainbow in the sky,
And, tho' in science but a child,
He saw with gladden'd heart, and eye.

And so, I apprehend, that we
Should oft restrain our thoughts and sight,
Nor delve too far, nor try to see,
With deeper, but more painful light.

B

NIAGARA FALLS.

NIAGARA, thou mighty flood,
I've seen thee fall, I've heard thee roar,
And on the frightful verges stood,
That overhang thy rocky shore.

I've sailed o'er surging waves below,
And view'd the rainbow's colour'd light,
And felt the spray, thy waters throw,
When leaping, with resistless might.

I've seen the rapids in their course,
Like madden'd, living things rush on,
With wild, unhesitating force,
To where thy mighty chasms yawn.

And there to take the awful leap,
And fall, with hoarse and sullen roar,
Into th' unfathomable deep,
Which rolleth on, from shore to shore.

Niagara, thou'rt mighty, grand,
Thou fill'st human souls with awe,
For thee, and for that mighty Hand,
Which maketh thee, by nature's law.

Thou'rt great, thou mighty. foaming mass
Of water, plunging, roaring down,
But so are we, yea, we surpass
Thee, and we wear a nobler crown.

Thy mighty head is crowned with foam,
And rainbows wreathe thy robes of blue;
Our earthly forms—our present home—
Are insignificant to you.

But look, thou mighty thund'rer, thou,
Tho' puny be our forms to thine,
These forms possess, yea, even now,
A spark, a ray of life divine,

Rush on, O waters! proudly hurl
Thyself to roaring depths below,
And let the mists of ages curl,
And generations come and go.

But know, stupendous wonder, know,
Thy rocks would crumble, at the nod
Of Him, who lets thy waters flow;
Thy Maker, but our Friend and God.

Thy rocks *shall* crumble, fall they must;
Thy waters, then, shall plunge no more,
But we shall rise, e'en from the dust,
To live upon another shore.

A SABBATH MORNING IN THE COUNTRY.

'TIS morning, and the meadows yet,
Are wet with gracious drops of dew.
Each blade of grass, and flow'r, is set
With sparkling gems of richest hue.
The sun, with rising glory, sheds
A radiance, that none divine,
Save those, who early leave their beds,
When glist'ning dew-drops briefly shine.

Just ere the rising sunbeams play,
From glorious orb, of rosy red,
There is no sound of life, no hum,
And but, seemingly, all things are dead.

But when the blessed, welcome beams,
Light up, and cheer, and warm the earth,
All things awaken from their dreams,
To celebrate Creation's birth.

The very fields are filled with life,
With hum of bee, and insect throng;
The woods are vocal, with the strife
Of friendly rivalry, in song.
But 'tis the Sabbath morn, and now
Are heard no sounds of industry,
Save milk-maid, calling to her cow,
Or buzzing of the toilsome bee.

Or save, perhaps, the gentle neigh
Of horses, answering the call,
For mother, father, child to-day
Must hear the holy words, that fall
From lips, that pray with them, and preach
To them, the old, old words of cheer.
They must receive the sounds, that teach
Those solemn truths, they love to hear.

But now, the sun's increasing heat
Hath dried the dew, and warm'd the air;
The feather'd songsters now retreat,
Fann'd by the sun's relentless glare.
The morning service now is o'er,
The pastor, kindly greeted too,
And, after greetings at the door,
They all their homeward way pursue.

JOHN AND JANE.

SAID Jane to John, " Come, let us wed,
    For know, dear John, I love you,
And, by the bright stars overhead,
    There's none I place above you."

"I doubt it not," said John, "and I
　　Reciprocate the feeling,
And here, with one despairing cry,
　　I kneel, and love you, kneeling."

"Then why, dear John, do you despair,
　　If you do love so madly?"
"Because," said John, "my pocket there
　　Is slim, and furnish'd badly."

"Oh, that is naught," said Jane, with glee,
　　"I'd marry you to-morrow,
And live on bread, and water free,
　　Without one grain of sorrow."

"All right," said John, "I'm with you there,
　　Old Logan's charming daughter,
You'll get the bread, the work to share,
　　And I will get the water."

————

THINGS MYSTERIOUS.

THIS earth's a mystery profound,
Its movements, make, and changes all—
A mystery which none can sound,
Who dwell upon the whirling ball.

And deeper far than all the rest,
Is man; a mystery unsolved
Since the first heave of ocean's breast,
Since the first course our earth revolv'd.

His thoughts, and e'en his actions too,
Possess a subtle meaning, when
That meaning others may construe,
As plain and open to their ken.

There is a place in every heart,
As secret as the silent tomb,
Where others have no lot nor part,
Where none may gaze, where none may room.

It seemeth strange, that flesh and blood
Should hold such ghostly, hellish things,
And also things supremely good,
Which might not shame an angel's wings.

Yet so it is, for ev'ry throb
That man's pulsating bosom gives,
And ev'ry smile, and ev'ry sob
Speaks of a mystery that lives.

There is a tale in ev'ry flow'r,
Which none may whisper, none may tell,
A secret thing in ev'ry bower,
Which ev'ry tenant hideth well.

There is a tale of joy and woe,
Round ev'ry hearth, in ev'ry land,
Which ne'er may ever further go,
Than round that humble, home-like band.

And shall we seek to draw the screen
Which hides the good, and eke the ill ?
No, it is better far, I ween,
To let them keep in hiding still.

For unknown good is virtue still,
And virtue shows a richer bloom,
As violet, or daffodil,
When growing 'mid the grass or broom.

And he who hides within his heart
A secret sin, all unconfess'd
To God or man, no glossing art
Can quiet the distracting guest.

THE PINE TREE.

THE wind last night was wild and strong,
   It shriek'd, it whistl'd and it roar'd,
And went with whirl and swoop along,
   'Mid falling trees and crashing board.

The timbers creak'd, the rafters sway'd,
   And e'en some roofs, upheav'd and torn,
Came crashing to the earth, and laid
   Before the view, upon the morn.

The air seem'd like some monstrous thing,
   By its uncurbéd passion held;
Like dreadful dragon on the wing,
   So horribly it scream'd and yell'd.

Now venting a triumphant shout,
   And ever and anon a groan,
Like fiend from prison lately out,
   Or like unhappy chain'd one's moan.

There was a lofty pine I knew;
   Each morn and eve I passed it by;
To such a lofty height it grew,
   It caught at once each passing eye.

It stood alone, and proudly stood,
   With straight, and clean, and lofty stem;
All other trees it seemed to view,
   As though it scorn'd to live with them.

Full many a winter's snow had whirl'd
   About its base, and settl'd there,
And many an autumn mist had curl'd
   About its head, so high in air.

Full many a blast had spent, in vain,
   Its force, for, ever like a rock,
It stood each persevering strain,
   And long defied the tempest's shock.

But yesternight it crashing fell,
   And now, this morn, I see it lie.
I knew the brave old tree so well,
   A tear almost bedims my eye.

But brave old trees, like brave old men,
   .Must feel at last the fatal stroke,
That dashest them to earth again,
   Tho' lofty pine, or mighty oak.

I'll miss, old tree, thy lofty stem
   Outlin'd against the distant sky,.
But 'tis no gain to fret for them—
   For men, or trees, that fall and die.

AUTUMN.

THE grass is wet with heavy dew,
The leaves have changed their bright green hue,
   To brighter red, or golden;
The morning sun shines with a glow,
As bright and pure as long ago,
   In time yclept the olden.

One tree is cloth'd with scarlet dress,
And one, with brown leaf'd loveliness,
   Delights the eye that gazes ;
While others varied tints display,
But all, in beauteous array,
   Delight us, and amaze us.

We see the trees in beauty clad,
But still that beauty makes us sad,
   E'en while we may admire,
For death has caus'd that sudden bloom
Stern death, the tenant of the tomb,
   Or funereal pyre.

The ruthless, bitter, biting air
Hath dried the life which flourish'd there,
   Throughout the warmer seasons ; .
The nourishment hath ceas'd to flow
Through veins, where once it us'd to go—
   Hath ceas'd for diff'rent reasons.

And soon the leaves will strew the ground,
And whirl with rustling ardor round,
   Or lie in heaps together,
Their hues of red, of brown, of gold,
Will blacken, as they change to mould
   By action of the weather.

But leaves will grow where once they grew,
Will bud, and bloom, and perish too,
   The same as all the others,
As we through youth, and joy, and grief,
Must find at last a sure relief,
   As did our many brothers.

Like in the leaf, no life-blood flows,
When frosts of death the fountain close,
   From which it flow'd, to nourish.
And like the leaf, another spring
Around us shall her gladness fling ;
   Another life shall flourish.

Our bodies turn to dust or mould.
As lifeless as the rocks, and cold,

But life's fair Tree is living.
And fadeless green leaves we shall be,
Because the Fountain of that Tree
 Eternal life is giving.

CHRISTMAS.

OLD father Time, his cruel scythe
 Has swung full oft around,
Since last the merry Christmas bells
 Rang out their cheerful sound.
With cruel vigor he has held
 His great, impartial sway,
And many thousands mown to earth,
 Who saw last Christmas day.

For some have left this world for aye,
 Who dwelt with us last year;
Glad voices heard amongst us then,
 We never more shall hear.
But still we'll build our Christmas fires,
 And sing our Christmas songs,
And for one day forget our griefs,
 Our failures and our wrongs.

Then ring, ye joyful bells, ring out;
 Ye crashing cymbals fall;
And for old Christmas, hale and stout,
 Sound up, ye harps and all.
Let music's loud and sweetest strain
 Beat from our hearts each ill;
Let thoughts of those assuage our pain,
 Who are around us still.

Oh, winsome maid, oh, hearty youth,
 I urge you on to glee,

For, in your innocence and truth,
  You all are dear to me.
Nor youth, nor age should cherish gloom,
  And voices oft should sing,
So give the gladsome voices room,
  And let the joy-bells ring.

CANADA.

COME now, my Muse, do thou inspire my pen,
To sing, with worthy strain, my country's praise,
But not to hide the faults within my ken,
By tricks of art, or studied, verbal maze,
To play on him who reads with careless gaze,
To whom each thought upon a printed page.
Is gospel truth, nor e'er with wile betrays ;
From this, oh, steer me clear, nor let the rage
Of prejudic'd and narrow minds, my thoughts engage.

Oh, Canada! the land where first I saw
The blue of heav'n, and bursting light of day,
Where breezes warm and mild, and breezes raw,
First o'er my boyhood's eager face did play,
As o'er the hills I stepp'd my joyful way.
Held by a loving hand, I went along
Thro' shelter'd wood, or by some shaded bay,
And ever, as I went, I sang a song,
With sylvan joy, amid a sylvan throng.

For birds and bees, and e'en the flowers, did sing
Their cheerful songs, with voices pure and sweet ;
Their notes were silent, yet those notes did bring
A soothing balm, amid a calm retreat.
Protected from the sun's relentless heat.

Oh, wearied men, could ye but once divine
The healing pow'r of some lone country seat,
You would not strive to drown your care in wine,
Or vainly seek relief, in any lustful line

But this is not a moralizing lay,
Of Canada I sing, and her alone,
Her varied progress, every passing day,
Her faults, for which, in time, she must atone,
By nature's law, in every clime and zone.
Then what are the peculiar, common claims,
Our country has with nations larger grown,
And the superior things she classes as her own.

First let us take her climate; who will not
Say she is favour'd there o'er other lands ?
The winter's cold, indeed, and summer's hot,
But in a robust health the native stands,
So keen to work with brain, or use his hands.
Where, let me ask, between the distant poles
Is there a clime so mod'rate in demands,
Where men are not compell'd to live like moles,
Nor drop with heat on burning, barren, sandy knolls.

A hardy, energetic, toilsome race,
Is raised within this favourable clime,
In physical and mental power apace
With those of any land, and any time,
Save in the golden age, that age of thought sublime;
But, what I mean is this : that her own men
Do act their parts, they reason or they rhyme
Within their bounds, with keen, far-reaching ken,
For those who late have left the axe to wield the pen.

Yes, left the axe, whose skilful, cleaving stroke
Hew'd out a home from 'mid the forest wild,
Where grew the maple and the lofty oak,
Where liv'd the dusky colour'd forest child,
So sternly fierce in war, in peace so mild ;

Yes, here the settler met with Nature's force;
Quite unsubdued, she look'd around and smil'd,
And seem'd to view with scorn the white man's course
Of labour slow, but yet of wealth the only source.

But still the patient white man plodded on,
He swung his axe, and drove his hornéd team;
At times he felt despair, but soon 'twas gone,
And gladsome rays of hope would brightly gleam
To cheer his path, like light on darken'd stream.
Some saw their hopes fulfill'd, some sank to rest
Amid their toil, but, sinking, saw the beam
Of brighter days, to make their children blest.
And give a rich reward to ev'ry earnest guest.

These latter gaz'd on fertile fields, and saw
The waving grain, where stood the forest tree,
Where prowl'd the bear; or wolf, with hungry maw,
Howl'd in the settlers' ears so dismally,
That children crouch'd near to their mother's knee.
They saw, instead of plain, bark-roof'd abode,
A mansion wide, the scene of youthful glee,
And happy Age, now resting on his road,
To pay the debt, his sinning kind so long hath ow'd.

The organ or piano sounds its tone,
Where late in darkness cried the whip-poor-will,
Or gloomy owl's to whoo! to whoo! alone,
Came from the glen, or darkly wooded hill.—
These sounds, untaught, and unimprov'd in skill.
All round, where'er they look, they see a change,
By rolling lake, by river, mount or rill;
Wherever feet may walk, or eyes may range,
There is a transformation pleasing, new and strange.

Schools, churches, built in costly, solid style,
Proclaim the fact that here a higher life
Is liv'd than that of seeking all the while

For wealth, and pow'r, amid ignoble strife,
Degrading unto husband, son or wife.
The scholar's light, and blest religion's smile
Ennobles, soothes and lends a joy to life—
A pow'r, which counteracts the trickster's wile
And blunts the edge of slander undeserv'd and vile.

From where the fierce Atlantic waters rage,
Unto the mild Pacific's fertile shore,
Small villages to cities rise and wage
A steady war; but not a war of gore—
A friendly rivalry exists, no more,
Save in the far North-West, where savage clan
Ungrateful rise, and make a serious sore,
Whose pains increas'd, as eastward far it ran,
And plac'd the British race beneath the Frenchman's ban.

But quickly, let us hope, the time may come,
When peacefully the British flag shall wave,
And when the rebels' terrorizing drum
Shall be as still as Riel's rebel grave,
O'er the wide land, whose sides two oceans lave;
When demagogues of party shall retire,
Or curb their selfish zeal, their land to save
From factious feuds and savage rebel fire.
And all that tends to raise the patriot's scorn and ire.

From ocean unto ocean runs a band,
A double band of hard and gleaming steel;
It binds in one this fertile, mighty land,
In bonds which all should recognize and feel,
If anxious to promote their country's weal.
A bond which Nature's sympathetic law
Should fasten on our hearts with solid seal,
Which factious feuds should ne'er asunder draw,
Nor wily traitors cut, by selfish treason's saw.

The strange, stupendous, magic power of steam,
In works, is great as fam'd Aladdin's ring,
It carries men o'er miles of land and stream,
And maketh loom and forge, with labour sing,
And o'er the land, a busy air doth fling.
That fluid, too, that none can well define,
In active life hath wrought a wondrous thing.
It speeds our words with lightning flash or sign,
And maketh glorious light from midnight's darkness shine.

Then to our country's future we may gaze
With gladden'd eyes, and hearts with hope aglow,
That our young country still its head will raise,
And stand 'mid nations, in the foremost row,
High honour'd there, and honour'd not for show—
For solid worth, and lasting pow'r and fame
Will be her portion, if her footsteps go
In duty's path, and if the ruddy flame
Of honor shines within, and keeps away all shame.

YOUTHFUL FANCIES.

THE morning of a gladsome day in spring
Had scarce its freshness brought to weary men,
When, o'er the meadows wet, a boy did sing,
And whistled o'er a tune, and carroll'd it, again,
In youthful happiness unconcious then
Of aught which time might bring, of pain or woe,
But careless, pitching stones in bog or fen,
It seem'd as if he buried there, also,
All worldly cares, so blithely did he onward go.

And yet he was no careless, heedless boy,
Who thought but of the present time alone.
Of future years he thought, but with such joy,
His thoughts but pleasure gave, nor caused a groan

From out the breast that claim'd them as its own ;
His thoughts were of the future, fair and bright,
And fresh from his unburden'd heart, alone,
Untarnish'd by the hard and glaring light,
By which he yet might see with such a diff'rent sight.

A picture of the blissful future, he
Had gaily painted in his youthful mind,
And thought no color there too bright to be
An image of his share from fortune kind,
Which she, in future years, would give so free,
To him, the lucky sailor on life's sea.
He thought of honor, happiness and fame,
As he went gaily o'er the dewy lea,
And to his mind no thought of failure came,
To win a prize of worth, in life's tremendous game.

He heard his parents, brothers, sisters, all,
With pride and fondness, speak his honor'd name,
And listen'd, while a nation's mighty call
Invited him to honor and to fame,
And crowds his praises shout, with loud acclaim ;
He saw in wealthy town his mansion wide,
And in the country view'd his fields, the same,
Until, in rapture, he had almost cried,
" In happiness and wealth all others are outvied."

He saw a lovely maiden by his side,
Who soon with him his favor'd lot would share,
He saw her upward glance of joy and pride,
As to his eyes she rais'd her face so fair,
So proudly glad that he, her lord, was there.
And all unconscious of her own sweet grace,
But, confident in his protecting care,
She gave him first within her mind the place,
And raised him high above all others of his race.

And now, how joyful rings the marriage bell,
Upon the brightest morn in his career.
He proudly hears the mighty organ swell,
While orange buds, and bridal robes, appear,
And people stop, the merry notes to hear.
And now the organ peals its parting strain,
And, issuing forth, they hear a stirring cheer,
While crowds surround the stately marriage train,
To cheer him and his bride, and cheer them once again.

These are the thoughts that fill his boyish mind,
And agitate and fire his youthful breast,
'Oh, why should fortune oft' be so unkind,
And real life appear in sombre colors drest,
And dash to earth bright hopes, and give so much unrest?
Oh, why should boyish hopes, and maiden's dreams
Fail, sadly fail, to stand the crucial test?
Say, why should all the brightness of man's schemes
Full often fade away, like earth's forgotten themes?

Why do you ask, O sad inquirer? How
Can things like that be known to mortal ken?
Suffice it, that it suits the mortal Now,
And leads our thoughts to the eternal Then,
When darkness shall be light, to ransom'd men,
When dreams of bliss, with glad fruition crown'd,
And happiness, untold by prophet's pen,
Shall fill the hearts of those who sought and found
That peace, which lighted up, and cheer'd life's weary
round.

HAPPINESS.

Fair Happiness, I've courted thee,
And used each cunning art and wile,
Which lovers use with maidens coy,
To win one tender glance or smile.

C

Thou hast been coy as any maid,
So lofty, distant, stern and cold,
And guarded from a touch of mine,
As miser guards his precious gold.

To win a smile from thee, did seem
A painful, fruitless thing to try,
Thy scornful, thin and cruel lips,
No pity gave thy steely eye.

Thy countenance, so sternly set,
Did seem to say how vain to knock
At thy heart's door, for all within
Was hard, as adamantine rock.

Thus unto me thy visage seem'd,
But faces do not always tell
The feelings of the heart within,
Or thoughts that underneath them dwell.

For e'en at times, I saw thy face
Relax, and look with pity down,
On struggling, weary mortals here,
Without one scornful glance or frown.

At times I've seen thy steely eye,
Sheath'd with a look of tender love,
As if thou saw our mortal woes,
And fain would help, but dare not move.

As if some higher power than thine,
Directed all things here below,
And for some wise and happy end,
Let struggling mortals suffer woe.

Except at times, when from thy face,
A cheerful light is shed on men,
And when, withdrawn within thyself,
We, hopeful, watch for it again.

Such is the happiness of earth,—
A sudden light, a glancing beam,·
Which cheers us in our lonely bark,
Upon times dark, relentless stream.

The stormy waves roll darkling on,
And with the current we must go,
Perchance to meet some cheerful beams
Of happiness, amid our woe.

But, if we guide our bark aright,
And guard the precious tenant there,
We soon shall reach a sea of light,
From this dark, troubl'd stream of care.

Then, may we never let the shade
Of bitter trouble and despair,
Hide from our eyes the happy gleams,
Which even we, at times, may share.

LOVE.

THOU source of bliss, thou cause of woe,
Disturber of the mind of man,
Wilt thou still calmly onward go,
A sightless leader of the van?

In court and camp wilt thou still rule,
And nation's destinies still sway;
Make wise men act as doth the fool,
And blindly follow thee, away?

Thou siren nymph, ethereal sprite,
Thou skilful charmer of mankind,
Oh, when wilt thou lead man aright,
And when will they thy cords unbind?

Thy potent spells have still their force,
And reason's dictates still are scorn'd,
And reason runs a shackl'd course,
While life, with love, is still adorn'd.

Thou fond inmate of maiden's breast,
Thou lighter up of manly heart;
Thou surely hast some high behest,
And we shall surely never part.

We'll never part, but oh, thou friend
And cheerer of life's dreary way.
May reason guide us to the end,
And may she ever with thee stay.

HATE.

WHILE love inspires, and friendship warms
    All hearts, in ev'ry state,
High over thee, grim hatred storms,
    As pitiless as fate.

Remorseless, unrelenting, hard,
    It holds its stubborn way,
Which duty's claim cannot retard,
    Nor righteous thoughts delay.

With steady look, it keeps its eye
    Fixed firmly on its foe;
With panting zeal it hurries by,
    To make its deadly throw.

In bosoms white it sits in state,
    And often, faces fair
Conceal the rankling fire of hate,
    Which looks may not declare.

It is not strange to church or state,
  For oft beneath the gown
Of prelate grave, and judge sedate,
  It sits with hideous frown.

Disturbing truth and righteous law,
  It scorns the bitter tear,
And laughs at all we hold·in awe,
  And all that causes fear.

O God of love, and not of hate,
  Look down where'er we be,
And snatch us, ere 'tis yet too late,
  From hate's black, raging sea.

From rolling tides of vengeful thought,
  Oh, lift us far above,
And may we thank Thee as we ought,
  From pleasant seas of love.

DISPLAY.

DEEP planted in the heart of man,
  Wherever you may go,
Display hath fertile seeds, which sprout,
  And daily larger grow.

As oftentimes,·in happy soil,
  A lofty tree may rise,
And 'neath its gloomy, blighting shade,
  A sprout, fair, tender, dies.

One lovely sprout, yes, more than one
  Droops, dies beneath the shade,
And, where might be a garden plot,
  A tangl'd waste is made.

Ill favor'd weeds, and poison'd fruit,
  In rank luxuriance reign,
And virtuous plants may strive to grow,
  But strive to grow in vain.

Oh, man, why in thy foolish heart
  Should one seed grow so well,
That naught but chaos there should reign,
  'Mid poison plants of hell.

Oh, man, immortal in thy soul,
  Thou dost possess a will,
Then why not prune these noxious sprouts,
  With firm and steady skill.

If thou would'st make thy heart a plot,
  ˙Trimm'd, bright, and pure, and clean,
Oh, let no tree o'erpow'r the rest,
  Or rank o'ergrowth be seen.

THOUGHT.

The blight of life, the demon, Thought.—BYRON.

WITH demon's shriek or angel's voice,
'Mid hellish gloom, or heav'nly light,
Thought haunts our path o'er land and sea,
And dwells with us, by day and night.

In roomy hall, or narrow hut,
It withers, blasts and kills with gloom,
Or gently onward smooths the path
Of him, who gives the tyrant room.

With siren voice it soothes our woe;
It dwells with us in blissful dreams;

But when we wake, it tells us then,
That it is far from what it seems.

Rebellious o'er its prostrate slave,
Its iron chain of bondage swings,
Or, govern'd by a master hand,
In numbers loud and strong, it sings.

And, with its keys of rarest mould,
Its stores of hoarded wealth unlocks,
It dives for man beneath the sea,
And cleaves for him the hardest rocks.

Forever thus it lives and acts,
With angel host, or demon throng,—
To sing with voice of heav'nly love,
Or shout, with dismal, hellish song.

Thus shall it live, thus shall it act,
While ages shall their cycles roll;
It leaves us when we reach the grave
But oh? it rises with the soul.

And still it lives in that beyond,
As here it lives in this our sphere,
To light our road and cheer our path,
Or torture us with nameless fear.

PURITY

KEEP pure the thoughts within thy mind,
    For they to actions turn,
Which succor want, or pity woe,
    Or all but self they spurn.

FAREWELL.

Keep pure thy thoughts, for outward looks
  Will then in beauty shine;
Although thy face be plain, 'twill be
  A human face divine.

Keep pure thy thoughts by trust in God,
  And, when in trouble's sea,
Look thou for strength to brave the storm,
  Upon thy bended knee.

Then lift thy head with fearless front,
  For come whatever may,
Thou'lt gather strength to brave it well,
  Thro' ev'ry passing day.

Keep pure thy heart, oh, keep it pure,
  And thou wilt bless the hour,
When thou withstood temptation's siege,
  And bridl'd passion's pow'r.

FAREWELL.

FAREWELL! and know, where'er I roam,
  My heart still turns to thee,
From spacious halls, or trackless woods,
  Or on the foaming sea.

Farewell, my friend! oh, could I say,
  My love, my own, to you,
My outlook on this dreary world
  Would have a brighter hue.

But duty calls, and I must go,
  E'en now, with outstretch'd hand,
I take a sad, sad leave of thee,
  To dwell in distant land.

For thy sweet sake I'll onward toil,
  In earnest, patient strife.
Content, if thou shalt know I live
  An earnest, useful life.

And if, in future years thou'rt free,
  And none has gain'd thy heart,
Oh, darling, wilt thou come to me,
  And we shall never part.

My shatter'd life will then be sweet,
  My spirit shall rejoice,
And weariness forsake my frame,
  At thy dear, loving voice.

Farewell! farewell! and oh, the words
  Dwell on my falt'ring tongue;
Oh, sad, despairing accents now,
  That from my lips are wrung.

O, God, look down in gracious love,
  And, for my pray'rs and tears,
Oh! guide and bless that gentle maid,
  Through all the coming years.

And, if on earth we meet no more,
  Grant, in thy boundless love,
That I till death may faithful be,
  And meet with her above.

IRELAND.

Thou green isle of sorrows, I think of thee daily,
  And sad are the thoughts that come into my brain,
When here, to my home, o'er the wide, rolling ocean,
  Is wafted the news of thy trouble and pain.

Oh, Erin ! I love thee in spite of thine errors,
    And now for thee, Erin, my heart is forlorn,
Disturb'd as thou art by such various terrors,
    Thou beautiful isle, where my kindred were born.

E'en now, in my thoughts, I can climb thy steep mountains,
    Or roam through thy valleys, where green shamrocks
      grow,
Or over thy meadows, where hedges of hawthorn
    Stand gracefully clipp'd, an impassable row.
And I see the thatch'd cottage, where often, the stranger,
    With kind word of welcome, is met at the door ;
The castle or tow'r, a shelter from danger,
    When foemen invaded thy sea-beaten shore.

Oh, Erin, I roam, in my thoughts, by thy rivers,
    I stand by thy lakes, in delight at the view,
And ever I pray for the time, that delivers
    This nation from strife, and from misery, too.
From Shannon's green banks unto Erne's limpid waters,
    I've travell'd in thought, while this was my pray'r :
That sons of Fermanagh, and Limerick's daughters.
    Should join in a union of loyalty, there.

For what loyal maid, from the banks of the Shannon,
    Or what Irish lad, from the slopes of the Bann,
Would not dread the day, when the boom of the cannon
    Should speak of destruction and death, from the van ?
And what loyal son of old Ireland's glory,
    From Cork's cove of beauty, to Foyle's distant shore,
Would not mourn the day, when, cold, lifeless and gory,
    Brave forms downfallen, should rise never more ?

And who would not hail, throughout Erin's dominion,
    The time when Religion's bright form should arise,
And sail o'er the land, with her blest, healing pinion,
    And bring to all hearts the truth in one guise ?

And then, in his home, afar o'er the ocean,
  Or by the turf fire, upon Erin's old sod,
Each Irishman, kneeling in humble devotion,
  Would love all his brothers, while praying to God.

Oh Erin, mavourneen! Let Love's joyous fingers
  Strike out from your harps, one glad, resonant strain,
And, if one discordant, harsh, jarring note lingers,
  Oh, strike for your country, together again!
And then, when your hands and your hearts are united,
  When you kneel at one shrine, when you bow to one
    law.
With a sea of glad brightness, your isle shall be lighted,
  While thunders the chorus, of Erin-go-bragh.

BY THE LAKE.

THE waves are dashing on the shore,
  With wild, glad joy, I stand and view them;
And, as they break with sullen roar,
  My heart responds with gladness, to them

They've pow'r to thrill the human soul,
  As on the shore they break so madly,
The spirit, bounding, hears their roll,
  And speaks responsive, wildly, gladly.

The heart, with proud, defiant beats,
  Re-echoes the triumphant roar,
And, as each wave its course retreats,
  The pulse retires to beat once more.

The gull screams wildly o'er the waves,
  Defiant in its stormy glee;
It screams, perchance, o'er wat'ry graves
  And recks not, heeds not, nor do we.

But comes a time, when waves and wind,
   In restful quietude remain,
A change then comes upon the mind,
And stormy passion's recent reign.

The gull sails softly thro' the air,
   For all is calm and still below;
Peace, blessed peace is ev'rywhere,
   And all regret the recent throe.

The man, remorseful, thinks of how
   Defiant thoughts reign'd wild and high,
The waves are mourning, sobbing now,
   In peace, but yet in agony.

LOUIS RIEL.

MISGUIDED man, thy turbid life
   This day in shameful death shall close,
And thou shalt ne'er behold the sun,
   That in thy sight, this morn, arose.

The moon, which yestere'en so clear,
   Shone thro' thy cell's small window pane—
No more shalt thou behold its light,
   Or see its chasten'd rays, again.

No more thy voice, 'mong savage hordes,
   Shall sound, with baneful, potent spell,
To make them rise with savage force,
   And 'gainst their country's laws, rebel.

And thou art calm in trustful hope,
   And conscience gives thee little pain,
'Tis strange, but man's a myst'ry deep,
   Unsolv'd in finite thought's domain.

The scaffold's there, and thou art firm ;
　Thou walkest forth upon it now ;
The thoughts within thy breast are hid,
　But calm and peaceful is thy brow.

The man of God, thy faithful friend
　Of brighter days, and happier years,
Upon thy cheek, with holy lips,
　A kiss imprints, 'mid blinding tears.

The priest and thou art praying now,
　For thy poor soul, before 'tis gone,
When suddenly, with crashing force,
　The door descends—the bolt is drawn.

And what can be the pray'r of those,
　Who learn'd with awe thy dreadful death ?
It is that thou God's mercy found,
　Before thou yielded up thy breath.

It is that thou that mercy found,
　Which thou to others never gave ;
That thy rebellious, restless soul,
　A pardon found, beyond the grave.

Man's justice had to take its course,
　And tie the fatal hempen knot,
For vengeance cried from out the ground,
　Where lay the blood of murder'd Scott.

But who shall say e'en such a cry
　Did drown the voice of pard'ning love,
Which comes to sins of deepest dye,
　From Him who died, but reigns above ?

LINES ON THE NORTH-WEST REBELLION.

THE war is o'er, and vict'ry crowns
　　Our youthful soldiers brave,
And back their homeward steps have turn'd,
　　Save those who found their grave ;
Save those whom rebel bullets fell'd,
　　Whose martial souls have gone,
Whose bodies rest beneath the plains
　　Of wide Saskatchewan.

Sleep on, brave hearts ! Nor bugle sound,
　　Nor beat of martial drum
Shall make you spring to arms again,
　　And to your comrades come.
Sleep on, brave hearts ! Nor western storm,
　　Nor rebel balls you'll feel ;
You fought the last campaign of life,
　　And fought it well, with Riel.

And others wounded in the strife,
　　Their valor still will burn,
And to the bloody field again,
　　Their spirits brave return ;
Tho' maim'd, and bruis'd, and battle worn,
　　Their names are honor'd here,
Next to the names of those who fought,
　　And found a bloody bier.

Oh, British troops are brave,
　　To charge the foreign guns,
And British spirit shows itself
　　In our young country's sons.
Long, long may truth and valor strong,
　　Inspire Canadian hearts,
To meet with steady bravery,
　　All rebel balls and darts ;

To meet all foreign foes, or quell
  The sinful rebel's pride,
And teach that right must yet prevail,
  That justice must preside;
That law must ne'er be set at naught,
  By selfish cliques or clans,
That right must ne'er give way to might,
  That liberty is man's.

THE TEACHER.

SAY, sadden'd mortal, thou who goest along
With look so weary, and with step so slow,
Why trillest thou no blithe and cheerful song,
Why whistlest thou that tune, so sad and low?

What trouble weighs thee down, what sorrow sore
Lies heavy on thy yet so youthful breast?
Sure fortune yet holds wide for thee her door;
Sure fame and joy yet wait thy earnest quest.

Why, know'st thou not the birds for thee do sing,
The flow'rs for thee with perfum'd beauty grow,
With melody for thee the wild birds sing,
With rippling laugh, the cheerful streamlets flow?

Then why, my friend, once more I ask of thee,
Why shows thy face so much unrest and pain?
What painful phase of life dost thou still see?
What sad, sad woe, doth in thy heart remain?

Bright flash'd the teacher's languid eye,
Flushed his pale cheek, with bright, tho' fleeting flame;
Leap'd forth his voice with energetic cry,
And thus, to me express'd, his thoughts they came.

"Inquirer, cease, thy words stir up the fire,
  That erst did fill my live and vig'rous brain ;
Thy words stir up the seeds of healthy ire,
  That still, with latent pow'r and force, remain.

"'Tis strange, thou think'st, that darkly on my brow
  The shadow of a careworn spirit stays;
My youth, with springless step, doth make thee bow
  Thy head, in kindly wonder, and amaze.

"Thou would'st not look with such a puzzl'd air,
  Upon my weary pace, and heavy eye,
If thou didst know the cause of my despair,
  The stern, substantial, solid reason why.

" Didst ever know, my friend, what I endure,
  In slavish, plodding work, from day to day,
Which work should be in its own nature pure,
  And lifted high, from gross and heavy clay.

"Examinations, cram and pressure high,   .
  Are daily kept before my anxious mind ;
What tho' for higher aims I daily sigh,
  This is my work, and this my daily grind.

"I work, you say, on minds, and hearts, and souls,
  Alas, 'tis true, but what can e'er atone
For dry, mechanic thought, and lifeless coals,
  Which light not up, but turn the intellect to stone ?

" Work on ! ye faithful, grinding and hair-splitting band,
  Work on, in slavish fear, and penitential pain,
But daily pray, that thro' this young and prosp'rous land,
  A system, higher, purer, freer, yet shall reign.

" Yours shall not be the blame, the people must it bear,
  For, while they look for quick results, for hot-bed flow'rs,
Amongst them, they the various ills must surely share,
  Of hasty fev'rish work, compell'd by outside pow'rs."

Thus spoke the man, and closed his lips became,
The fire forsook his lately flashing eye,
His nerves relax'd, and o'er his brow, the same
Dark cloud of bitter woe, could I descry.

THE INDIAN.

WHEN wooded hill, and grassy plain,
　　With nature's beauties, gaily dress'd,
Lay calm beneath the red man's reign,
　　And smiling, in unconscious rest,

Then roam'd the forest's dusky son,
　　In nature's wildness, proudly free,
From where Missouri's waters run,
　　Far north, to Hudson's icy sea.

From Labrador, bleak, lonely, wild,
　　Where seal, 'mid icebergs, sportive play,
Far westward wander'd nature's child,
　　And wigwam built, near Georgia's Bay.

With bow of elm, or hick'ry strong,
　　And arrow arm'd with flinty head,
He drew with practis'd hand the thong,
　　And quick and straight, the shaft it sped.

Full many a bounding deer or doe,
　　Lay victims of his hand and eye,
And many a shaggy buffalo,
　　In lifeless bulk did lowly lie.

The forest did his wants supply,
　　Content he was with nature's scheme ;
For, fail'd the woods to satisfy,
　　There came response from lake or stream.

D

His simple shell of birchen rind,
  Propell'd by skilful hands, and strong,
Down cataracts and rivers pass'd,
  And over lakes, it went along.

With spears, from stone or iv'ry, wrought,
  Or hooks, ingenious made of bone,
He stores from out the waters brought,
  Nor look'd for forest gifts, alone.

Contentment dwelt within his heart,
  And, from his dark and piercing eye
His freedom showed, unbred of art,
  His honor look'd unconsciously.

Untaught by books, untrain'd by men,
  Vers'd in the thoughts of bard or sage,
He yet had read from nature's hand,
  A book unwrit, yet wise its page.

One would have thought a man so bless'd
  And richly, too, with manly pow'rs,
Had surely some far higher quest,
  Than living thus, in nature's bow'rs.

One would have thought, that when he knew
  The laws of God, and cultur'd men,
His mind would take a nobler view,
  And light pursue, with eager ken.

But such is not his happy state,
  Since light of knowledge round him shone ;
He still stands sadly at the gate,
  And few still go, where few have gone.

And whose the fault, and whose the blame,
   That thus his mind is still so dim,
That wisdom's lamp, with shining flame.
   Still gives so pale a light, for him.

Oh, thinking white man, look around,
And, when you have discern'd the cause,
Express yourself with certain sound,
Concerning this poor forest child,
Who left his father's hunting ground.

TO NOVA SCOTIA.

Oh brothers, friends, down by the sea,
   We can thy voices hear,
And painful is their tone, and free,
   Upon each brother's ear.

We hear each voice, pitch'd strong and high,
   And, could we see you now,
Our hearts would heave another sigh,
   At each beclouded brow.

We hear thy voice, from day to day,
   In one long, doleful strain,
Oh tell us why, oh brethren say
   Why sounds that voice of pain.

Are we not one, in race and creed,
   Rul'd by one gracious queen ?
And we have all receiv'd our meed
   Of praise and pelf, I ween.

Why vex her now, who's rul'd so long
   Upon her virtuous throne ?
Why sing her such a doleful song,
   And send her such a groan ?

And why annoy that whiten'd head,
   Our land's adopted son,
Who wisely drew love's slender thread,
   And wedded us in one.

And firmer yet he wish'd to bind
   Us to our country's weal,
And see, plann'd by his master mind,
   One band of glitt'ring steel,

One shining track, which stretches far,
   From wild Columbia's shore,
To where those doleful voices are,
   And the Atlantic's roar.

Oh brethren, friends down by the sea,
   With us your voices raise,
Instead of groans, oh, shout with glee,
   With us, one shout of praise.

And trust him, brethren, trust us, too,
   Seek not from us to go ;
Our country's good is weal for you,
   And common, all our woe.

A SNOW STORM.

I HEAR the wintry wind again,
   . I see the blinding snow,
Pil'd high, by eddying winds, in heaps,
   No matter where I go.

The storm is raging hard, without ;
   But let us not complain,
For fiercely tho' it rages now,
   A calm will come again.

And, though the wildly raging storm
  Makes all things bleak and bare,
Beside the fire we brave it well,
  And closer draw our chair.

In social fellowship, our hearts
  With kindly thoughts grow warm ;
Then is there not a pleasant side,
  E'en to a raging storm ?

And when the angry storm has calm'd,
  As ev'ry storm must do,
Then, sure, the tempest's handiwork
  Has pleasant features, too.

An artist's eye would look around,
  Upon these calmer days,
And view the pure white heaps of snow,
  With pleas'd and puzzl'd gaze.

Like purest marble, deftly carv'd,
  They stretch o'er vale and hill,
Fair monuments, not made by man,
  But rear'd by nature's skill.

The sweeping curve, the graceful arch,
  The line so firm and free ;
A skilful sculptor well might say :
  " Can this teach aught to me ? "

The trees are rob'd in purest white,
  And gleaming atoms shine
From out the snow, beneath the sun,
  Like stones from Ophir's mine.

The merry shouts of busy men
  Sound, as they dig the snow ;
And, when the way is clear, the bells
  With joyful jingle, go.

Then who shall say the tempest's work
　　Brings more of pain than joy;
Or that the evil things, to us
　　Are pain, without alloy?

CATCHING SPECKLED TROUT.

In early days, when streams ran pure,
　　Untainted from their spring,
Unchok'd by sawmill dust, or logs,
　　Or any other thing,

Each river, creek and rill ran on,
　　So pure, and free, and bright,
That through the gloomy shades, they shed
　　A cheerful, happy light.

The finny tribes, of varied kinds,
　　Ran swiftly to and fro,
And with most swift and graceful dart,
　　The speckl'd trout did go.

So swift to dash, and quick to see,
　　He caught the fatal fly,
Before less active fishes had
　　E'en turn'd to it their eye;

For, ever active and alert,
　　At once, or not at all,
He caught the tempting bait he saw
　　Upon the waters fall.

These were the days to angler dear,
　　When, with his hook and line,
He brought his treasures from the brook,
　　So splendid and so fine,

Each angler had his fav'rite spot,
   Wherein he held his breath,
To watch the fishes rush and plunge,
   So sure to bring its death.

But now the angler rarely throws
   With great delight, his line,
Or listens to the rippling brook,
   Beside the wild grape vine.

The finny treasures now are scarce,
   In river, creek or rill,
For poison'd are they by the dust,
   That comes from lumber mill.

The picturesque and shady grove,
   Which streamlets hurried by,
Are now uncover'd by the sun;
   Full many a stream is dry.

The poet's land is going fast;
   Wild beauty must give place
To useful and substantial things,
   Which benefit our race.

But who shall e'er forget the joys,
   When, from some shady nook
He flung his fly, with practic'd hand,
   Far out upon the brook?

THE HUNTSMAN AND HIS HOUND.

When hill and dale, long years ago,
   Lay clad in nature's dress,
And flourish'd the primeval pomp
   Of nature's wilderness,

A huntsman and his hound would roam,
Where fed the timid deer,
And where the partridge's drum, or whirr,
Brought music to his ear.

In sooth, he heard all forest sounds
With real sportsman's joy ;
And here he always pleasure found,
With little of alloy.

The pigeon's coo, the squirrel's chirp,
The wild-bird's thrilling lay,
Brought freshen'd pleasure to his heart,
At ev'ry op'ning day.

But music sweeter far than aught
In wood or vale around,
Was the loud crackling of the deer,
Or baying of his hound.

Full many a deer his steady aim,
With faithful rifle slew,
But, faithful as his rifle was,
His hound was faithful, too.

With loud, sonorous bay, he ran
Through swamp, or darken'd brake,
Till, from the bush the deer would bound
Far out into the lake.

And then, with ready boat at hand,
The hunter got his game ;
For to its struggling, frightened mark,
The well-aim'd bullet came.

And thus they liv'd from day to day,
This hunter and his hound ;
With nature's simple joys content,
He felt not life's dull round.

A hunter's life he dearly lov'd,
   And still, from day to day,
No other sound he lov'd to hear,
   Like his own deer-hound's bay.

. But soon that voice must sound no more ;
   The faithful dog must die;
The man must hunt the deer, without
   That well-known, guiding cry.

The hound had chas'd a noble buck
   Right down into the lake,
But roll'd the waves so high and strong,
   The noble beast did quake

With fear, for now he saw 'twas death,
   To leave the solid shore—
A lesser danger there he saw,
   So back he came once more.

He came with fierce, determin'd bounds,
   Impell'd by wild despair,
With lower'd head he reach'd the dog,
   Who bravely met him there.

But short the fight, the antlers gor'd
   The dog's brave heart, so true
To him who stood upon the shore,
   As spell-bound by the view.

The dog's death yell rang o'er the lake,
   For him, and for his foe,
As whizzing came the well-aim'd ball,
   That laid the slayer low.

The bullet came, but yet too late
   To save the gallant hound ;
And long the hunter mourn'd his loss,
   And miss'd his voice's sound.

GRACE DARLING.

The steamer Forfarshire, one morn
　　Right gaily put to sea,
From Hull, in merry England,
　　To a Scottish town, Dundee.

The winds were fair, the waters calm,
　　And all on board were gay,
For sped the vessel quickly on,
　Unharrass'd in her way.

All trim and neat the vessel look'd,
　　And strong, while, from on high
Her flag stream'd gaily, over those
　　Who deem'd no danger nigh.

So strong she look'd from stem to stern,
　　That all maintained that she
Would weather e'en the fiercest storm,
　　From Hull unto Dundee.

But bitterly deceiv'd were they,
　　When off North England's shore,
The vessel in a nor'-west gale,
　　Did labor more and more.

Her timbers creak'd, her engines mov'd
　　With weak, convulsive shocks,
And soon the ship, beyond control,
　　Rush'd madly on the rocks,

And then a lighthouse keeper saw
　　Her struggle with the waves,
And knew that soon, if came no help,
　　They'd find them wat'ry graves.

" What boat," he said, "could pass to them
    O'er such a raging sea,
And e'en if I should venture out,
    Oh ! who would go with me" ?

" Oh father, I will go with you,
    Out o'er the raging sea ;
To rescue them, come life, come death,
    I'll work an oar with thee."

She went, and battling with the sea,
    They reach'd the vessel's side,
And sav'd nine precious lives,
    From sinking in the tide.

For those, who on the wreck remain'd,
    Afraid to trust the waves,
In such a frail and loaded boat,
    Soon found uncoffin'd graves.

All noble acts, unconsciously
    Are done, with pure intent ;
And thus, upon her errand bold,
    This noble maiden went.

And when, from many mouths, she heard
    Her praises told aloud,
'Twas but for simple duty done,
    This modest maid felt proud.

And when, into her lone abode
    Fam'd artists quickly came,
No swelling and self-conscious pride
    Did animate her frame.

They knew rewards would scarcely do,
    To tell what should be told,
And yet, they gave this modest girl
    Five hundred pounds in gold.

But gold her peerless bravery
  Could neither buy nor pay,
And yet, content, her lonely life
  She liv'd from day to day.

A DREAM.

ONE night, while peaceful in my bed
I lay, unwitting what befell,
By Morpheus' arms claspéd close,
In blissful rest, I slumber'd well.

When suddenly, unto my ears
There came a dreadful, piercing sound,
So strange unto my startl'd mind,
I left my bed with single bound.

And then, transfix'd unto the floor,
I stood, in terror pinion'd there,
With drops of sweat upon my brow,
And eyes with fix'd and rigid stare.

I listen'd for the dreadful sound,
Which brought such terror to my brain;
And then, with wildly beating heart,
I heard the fearful noise again.

Affrighted yet, I heard the noise,
Which, tho' 'twas modified in tone,
It terror brought unto my heart,
And from my lips it drew a groan.

For horror yet was in the sound,
That froze my blood, and fix'd my eye;
It seem'd to me a demon's shriek,
Or wailing banshee's boding cry.

But soon my eyes unfix'd their stare,
My senses clearer now became,
And borne unto my sharpen'd ear,
I heard a sound, but not the same.

Within the plaster'd wall, near by,
I heard a grinding, ringing tone—
A mouse was gnawing at a board;
That was the sound, and that alone.

I waited then, and listen'd long;
But naught there came unto my ear,
Save this, and lying down again,
I wonder'd what had caus'd my fear.

And then I thought 'tis thus with us—
We mortals, who, with darken'd sight
See things, and fearful sounds do hear,
Which cause our narrow senses fright.

But when we waken from this dream,
With senses join'd to earth no more,
Our brighten'd faculties will see
No fear, where fear there was before.

THE TEMPEST STILLED.

THE sky was dark with threat'ning clouds,
And fiercely on the raging sea,
The roaring tempest wilder swept,
And fiercer rag'd old Galilee.

Deep, dark and wild the waters roll'd,
And fast across the lurid sky
The black clouds pass'd, as if to hide
The lights of heav'n from human eye.

A little boat, from crest to crest
Was lash'd about, and wildly thrown,
While down below lay timid souls,
Too faint to shriek, too weak to groan.

While thunders roll'd, and lightning flash'd,
And fiercer onward rush'd the waves,
Deep down below these mortals look'd
With frighted mind, to wat'ry graves.

The helmsman held the rudder still,
But unavailing his control ;
The blasts grew wild, and wilder yet,
And louder grew the thunder's roll.

His hand grew faint, his heart grew sick,
As still he saw the lightning's glare,
And heard the thunders toll his doom,
And voices shriek it in the air.

Air, water, heavens, all combin'd,
Seem'd on the ship their wrath to pour,
Combin'd to sink it in the tide,
And keep it ever from the shore.

One hope was left, and only one ;
The Master on a pillow slept,
And to him these affrighted ones,
So weak of faith, in silence crept.

With gentle touch they wake the Lord,
And half in hope, and half in fear,
They cry, " O save us, or we're lost.
O Master, Lord, wilt thou not hear ? "

With gentle mien the Master rose,
And to his mild, but mighty will,
The thunders, winds and billows bow'd,
And answer'd yes, his " peace be still."

" O, fearful ones, why do you fear ? "
Then said the mighty Lord of all;
" Why trust ye not, ye faithless ones,
And call in faith, whene'er ye call ? "

Thus, on the raging sea of life,
While billows wild around us swell,
Let faith in Christ our fears disperse,
Let trust in Him our sorrows quell.

When bitter anguish fills our breast,
And weak and trembling grows our hand,
Give Christ the rudder of our ship,
And he will bring us safe to land.

For wind, and sea, and thunder's roll,
His great command at once obey,
And those who trust Him, He will lead
Through storm and gloom, to perfect day.

THE SCHOOL–TAUGHT YOUTH.

His step was light, and his looks as bright
   As the beams of the morning sun,
And his boyish dreams, as the rippling streams
   That gently onward run,
Without a shock from rugged rock
   To check their course of glee,
As they wound their way, day after day,
   To their destin'd goal, the sea.

He had come from the schools brimful of rules,
   His head and note-book cramm'd
With varied lore, from many a shore,
   Pack'd solid in, e'en jamm'd.

He'd learn'd a part of many an art,
   Had studied mathematics,
And thought he knew how people grew,
   In palaces or attics.

He'd scann'd the page of many a sage,
   And did his mind adorn
With classic sweets, and varied treats,
   Preserv'd ere he was born.
" And now," says he, " upon life's sea
   I'll steer my bark so truly ;"
"She is," he thought, "so trim and taut,
   She cannot prove unruly."

He look'd each morn, with cultur'd scorn
   On homely barks beside him,
And pass'd them by right merrily,
   Whenever he espied them.
"O do but note how well they float,"
   An aged man did say ;
He pass'd him by with flashing eye:
   " I've mark'd me out my way."

" And did you see how easily
   Those ships their helm obey'd,
When in that storm your vessel's form
   So near the rocks was laid.
Young man so stern, you've yet to learn
   That sailing on life's sea
Is not an art to get by heart,
   Just like the rule of three.

" You'll have to know this ' fleeting show,'
   Tho' fleeting it may be,
Requires tact to think and act,
   That is not known to thee."

Thus the old man said, but this youth so read
   In varied arts and lore,
Bent not his neck, but trod the deck,
   And calmly look'd on shore.

But soon the shore was seen no more,
   The sea, so calm, got troubl'd;
The billows wild, no more beguil'd,
   But round him boil'd and bubbl'd.
The craft it sway'd; the boy, dismay'd,
   Saw how she rode unsteady;
The helm in vain they tug and strain,
   For storms she is not ready.

She pitch'd and toss'd; she's lost! she's lost!
   For see the rocks beside her;
Each effort's vain; she's cleft in twain,
   And now, O woe betide her!
The old man spoke, as through her broke
   The cruel rocks around her.
" Advice was vain; you took the chain,
   And helplessly you bound her.

" For all your store of varied lore,
   Tho' guidance and defence,
Was quite in vain to stand the strain,
   Like rocks of common sense."

THE TRUANT BOY.

AFTER MOORE'S " MINSTREL BOY."

OH, the truant boy to the woods has gone,
And you ne'er, alas, can find him,
He's strapp'd his empty school bag on,
For his books are left behind him.

E

He's gone to shake the beechnuts down
From a height—'twould make you shiver,
And stain his hands a gipsy brown,
With the walnuts by the river.

" Away from school !" said this youth so free,
" Tho' all the world should praise thee,
I'd rather climb this walnut tree,
Because it's such a daisy."
The truant fell, but the stunning shock
Could not bring his proud soul under ;
" I'll try again, and here I go
To get those nuts, by thunder ! "

So he tightly strapp'd his bag so neat,
This soul of spunk and bravery,
And said, " If I in this get beat,
I will go back to slavery."
But he climb'd the tree, and got the nuts,
And wander'd home in the gloaming,
Well knowing, as the door he shuts,
That his pa, with rage, is foaming.

But he gets some bread, and steals to bed
With his heart fill'd up with sorrow,
And shudders, as he looks ahead,
And thinks of school to-morrow ;
He knows the score of lies he'll tell
Will scarce prevent a licking,
And he sadly wonders if 'tis well
To go thus walnut picking.

THE FISHERMAN'S WIFE.

THE fisherman's wife stood on the beach.
One chilly April day,
And far out on the lake she look'd,
And o'er the waves, away.

The ice which late had spann'd for miles
  This rolling, inland sea,
Had now releas'd its wintry grasp ;
  The long pent waves were free.

And now resistlessly they roll'd,
  And frightful was the sound,
As cakes of ice, dash'd to and fro,
  Against each other ground.

A north-west wind had lately lash'd
  The waves to fury wild,
But now they fast were sinking down,
  Like tam'd and frighten'd child.

The woman caught their soughing sound,
  As tho' she heard a groan,
And heard them roll upon the beach,
  With sad and solemn moan

For late, with wild, hilarious glee,
  Their reckless course had run,
And now, it seem'd as if they thought
  Of all the ill they'd done.

The fisherman's wife stood on the beach,
  And still her eyes did strain,
To catch of mast or sail, a glimpse,
  Upon the inland main.

The woman turn'd her from the beach,
  Loose flow'd her streaming hair,
And, louder than the white-rob'd gull,
  She shriek'd in wild despair.

Three days ago her husband had,
  For wife and children's sake,
Dar'd changeful gales and floating ice,
  Upon the treach'rous lake.

With two stout hearts he left the shore,
  To reach the fishing " grounds,"
Undaunted by the freezing winds,
  Or ice-floes crushing sounds.

They reach'd the grounds, but scarce had turn'd
  Upon the homeward track,
When came the wild nor'-wester down
  On their frail fishing smack.

Yes, wring your hands, thou fisher's wife,
  For thou hast cause to wail
For him who left the fishing " grounds "
  In that wild north-west gale.

'Mid frozen snow, and blocks of ice,
  And fiercely rolling waves,
He and his little crew went down,
  Uncoffin'd, to their graves.

YE PATRIOT SONS OF CANADA.

YE patriot sons of Canada,
  Whate'er your race or creed,
Arise, your country claims you now,
  In this, her hour of need.

Arise, with right and valor girt,
  To battle with the foe,
Which threatens to defy our laws,
  And lay our country low.

Arise, for black rebellion's flag,
　Again may 'mongst us wave,
And traitors in our country's camp,
　May dig our country's grave.

The law was righteously enforc'd,
　Riel did fairly die,
And why should we give way to those,
　Who raise the rebel's cry ?

In spite of priest's or statesman's voice,
　Quebec, forsooth, must rage,
And, with her wrongful acts and words,
　Insult experience and age.

And demagogues, with purpose vile,
　Must lead the trait'rous cause,
And hound unthinking masses on,
　To wreck our country's laws.

Then rise, each patriotic son,
　And guard your country's flag,
Both for your own and country's sake,
　Oh, never let it drag.

By vote, and action, if there's need,
　Assert your country's claim,
To brandish high stern Justice' sword,
　O'er any race or name.

Arise then, sons of Canada,
　In purpose strong and bright,
Fear not the foe, nor doubt results,
　For God defends the right.

A PROTESTANT IRISHMAN TO HIS WIFE.

" Just forty years to-day, my dear,
   We sail'd from Irish waters,
And bade farewell, with many a tear,
   To Erin's sons and daughters.

" You'll recollect how ach'd our hearts,
   That day in Tipperary,
When we set forth for foreign parts,
   For distant woods or prairie.

" You know our very hearts were rent
   With grief, almost asunder,
And if we thought all joy was spent,
   No exil'd heart will wonder.

" But soon we reach'd our strange, new home,
   Where mighty forests flourish'd,
With others, forc'd like us to roam,
   Who in our isle were nourish'd.

" But now I'm fairly happy here,
   And so are you, my Mary,
But still I've seen you drop a tear
   Betimes, for Tipperary.

" We've many friends from home, here, now,
   And some we call our brothers,
While some we meet with clouded brow,—
   Their creed, our feeling smothers.

" There's some from Dublin, Cork, indeed
   There's some from distant Galway,
But ev'ry man, whate'er his creed,
   Should own his country, alway.'

" Tho' one attends the church, and one
  Devoutly seeks the chapel,
Agreeably they yet might run,
  Nor have one discord apple.

" True Irishmen have often met,
  One common cause to feel,
And many a furious onset met,
  With ' valor's clashing steel.'

" And surely there will come a day,
  When common thoughts and aims,
Will shed a pure and healthy ray,
  And show what duty claims.

" Sure Parson E. went o'er the sea,
  And back he came so smily,
With stick so fine from black-thorn tree,
  For father John O'Rielly.

" Thus we, as Irishmen, should ne'er
  Forget our common land,
Or claims of breth'ren, ev'rywhere,
  Upon our heart and hand."

NATURE'S FORCES OURS.

I SEE the wild and dashing waves
  Break madly on the shore;
With glee I watch their stately course,
  With joy I hear their roar.
The howling of the wildest storm,
  The shrieking of the gull
Drive quickly all of pain away,
  And all my fears they lull.

I join my feeble voice with theirs,
   Triumphant in its yell,
For evil powers of earth I scorn,
   And all the pow'rs of hell.
Tho' men and devils both unite,
   And all their force combine,
I feel, ye waves and howling winds,
   That all your strength is mine.

For He who holds you in His hand,
   And moulds you to His will,
Can whisper to all hostile pow'rs,
   As to you, " Peace, be still ! "
He bends your necks like osiers green,
   Also the necks of men ;
Therefore with you I raise my voice,
   And shout aloud, again.

For you are on my side, ye waves,
   And you, ye winds, are mine,
If I but cast off worldly cares,
   If I my will resign.
Then let me feel what I have felt
   Full oft, in days of yore—
A fearful, joyous pulse of life
   Thrill through me, at your roar.

Let me fling on your crests, ye waves,
   My loads of heavy woe,
And on your wings, ye howling winds,
   My cares and sorrows throw.

THE READING MAN.

With patient toil, from day to day,
  The printed page he scann'd,
The page of learnéd book, or sheet
  With news from foreign land.

And people thought him wond'rous wise,
  And he himself was vain
Of all the knowledge he had stor'd
  Within his jaded brain.

What other men were working at,
  He knew from day to day,
But never dream'd his barren task
  Was only idle play.

Fill'd with the thoughts of other minds,
  His words were barren, dry ;
He seldom coin'd a thought himself,
  He had so many by.

And when he found himself alone,
  Where self could only think,
He found the store withhin his brain,
  A weight to make him sink.

What he had always thought were ends,
  He saw were only means,
And, for his urgent purpose now,
  Were worth—a row of beans.

With loud and bitter voice he curs'd
  Newspapers, books and all,
That weaken'd his own manhood's force,
  And drove him to the wall.

He saw that man must be himself,
   Or he will live in vain,
That nothing in this world can take
   The place of his own brain.

The man who rides, but never walks,
   Should surely never pout,
If in a race he falls behind,
   Where horses are rul'd out.

The man who thinks by press or book,
   No matter how profound,
Will find a grave some day, beneath
   An ink and paper mound.

A VIRTUOUS WOMAN.

Proverbs, Chap. xxxi.

A WOMAN pure, oh, who can find ?
Her price is dearer far than gold,
And greater in her husband's mind,
Than shining gems, or pearls untold.

In her he safely puts his trust,
And while her life shall last,
His welfare she shall surely seek,
His honor holding fast.

With willing hands she works in flax,
In wool, and many other things,
And, rising early in the morn,
Her household's portion duly brings.

She buyeth fields, she planteth vines,
And girds herself to duty's round,
And far into the shades of night,
Her spindle plies with busy sound.

Her open hand, and gen'rous heart,
The poor and needy daily bless,
And in the cold her household walk,
All warmly clad in scarlet dress.

And she herself, in bright array
Of gorgeous silk and tapestries,
Brings gladness to her husband's face,
Who sits in honor 'mid the wise.

In honor and in virtue strong,
Her joy shall come in future days;
She speaks with gentleness to all;
The law of kindness guides her ways.

She governeth her household well,
And eateth not of idle bread,
Her husband gives the praise she earns,
Her children bless her worthy head.

Amid the virtuous and the good,
Of womankind she stands alone,
Unconscious of her priceless worth—
A queen on her domestic throne.

MAN.

ONE day I sat me down to write,
  And thought with might and main,
But neither subject fit, nor thoughts,
  Came to my barren brain.

And then I laid my pen aside,
  With sad, despairing mind,
And, fill'd with self-contemptuous scorn,
  I thought of human kind.

I saw a trifling, feeble race,
　　With narrow thoughts and aims,
Each noble aspiration crush'd
　　By rigid duty's claims.

Selfish and hard, they toil'd along,
　　And, in the bitter strife,
Neglected all that sweeten'd toil,
　　Or that ennobl'd life.

Another day I sat me down;
　　A happy subject came,
And pleasant thoughts light up my mind
　　With bright and cheerful flame.

And, as I thought, with heart aglow,
　　Self-satisfied I grew,
And guag'd with ampler girt, my mind,
　　And minds of others, too.

With satisfaction now, I view'd
　　Creation's mighty plan;
And had a clearer vision too,
　　And juster thoughts of man.

A toiling mortal yet, I saw,
　　But saw no more, a clod,
For far as mind o'er matter is,
　　He stood, plac'd by his God.

For now I saw to man was given
　　The right to rule and reign,
And bend all other pow'rs to his,
　　In nature's wild domain.

The light of endless life gleam'd forth
　　From his pain'd body's eye,
And tho' in shackles now it liv'd,
　　That light should never die.

The window now, thro' which it look'd,
　Might clos'd in darkness be,
But in a world above, beyond,
　Eternal light 'twould see.

And this is what I learn'd that day,
　When I sat down to write :
That man, above all earthly things,
　Sits plac'd by lawful right.

And tho' he lives this life below,
　'Mid accidents and pain,
There is a better life for him,
　When he shall live again.

And tho' his road upon this earth
　Be dusty, bleak and bare,
Another, and a joyful road,
　Is his, to travel there.

LIFE.

"WHAT is life ?" I asked a lad,
　As on with joyful bound,
He went to join the merry troop,
　Upon the cricket ground.

He paus'd at once with pleasant look,
　This bright-ey'd, laughing boy,
"Why, life," said he, " is sport and mirth;
　With me 'tis mostly joy.

"The tasks which I receive at school,
　I feel to be unkind;
But when I get my ball and bat,
　I drive them from my mind.

" With other boys I run and shout,
 I throw and catch the ball,
Oh, life is a right jolly thing,
 To take it all in all."

"And what is life ? " I asked a maid,
 Who trod, as if on air,
So lightly she did trip along,
 So bright she look'd, and fair.

The maiden stopp'd her graceful steps,
 And to my words replied,
" Oh, life's a lovely dream," she said,
 With some slight boons denied.

" But love, and health, and beauty crowns
 My lot so filled with cheer,
That joy beams forth from ev'rything,
 To favor'd mortals here.

" The birds and flow'rs are fill'd with joy,
 With joy the birds do sing ;
The very rain that comes from heav'n,
 Seems loads of joy to bring.

" And when I look to future years,
 The view seems brighter still,
And brighter grow the perfum'd flow'rs,
 As I go up the hill."

" And what is life ? " I asked a man,
 A man of middle years.
" This world is truly call'd," he said,
 " A vale of bitter tears.

"I thought this earth a bright, fair spot,
 But that was long ago;
I view it now, with truer sight,
 And see a world of woe.

"With disappointment and regret,
 And hopes thrown to the ground,
I live, but with an aching heart
 I tread life's weary round."

"And what is life?" This time a man
 With hoary hair replied.:
"This life consists of gracious boons,
 With evils by their side.

"To leave the bad, and choose the good,
 Is done but by the few,
And that is why mankind are such
 A discontented crew.

"With greed, the pleasure now is grasp'd,
 Or what they deem is so,
Not thinking that each pleasure now,
 May bring a future woe.

"My son, take heed to what I say,
 And see thou mark it well,
All earthly joys, too much indulg'd,
 Will lead you down to hell.

"For Heaven's sake, I pray you now
 To curb your youthful will,
Nor give your headstrong passions play,
 To use their deadly skill.

"There's joy, my son, all through this life,
    To meet, as well as woe,
And if mankind would act aright,
    Much more of it they'd know.

"With prudence, virtue, for your friends,
    And caution by your side,
And faith in God's o'erruling pow'r,
    Your life will calmly glide.

"Content to bear the ills you meet,
    Mix'd always with your joy,
For human prudence can't avert
    Some woes, which still annoy.

"Pray that your mind be strong and clear,
    And vigorous your frame,
Your heart inspir'd with love and fear
    For your Creator's name."

———

A HERO'S DECISION.

HE just had reached the time of life,
    When cares are felt by men,
But when they're strong to bear them well,—
    A score of years and ten.
"Heigh ho!" says he, "and this is life,
    The dream of earlier years,
In which we see so much of joy,
    And naught of bitter tears.

"I've lived a half a score of years,
    In search of fame and glory,
For all earth's boasted joys I've sought,
    But ah! what is the story?

The story ! 'tis the same old tale,
    Told long, long years ago,
But strange, each for himself must learn
    This earth's a ' fleeting show.'

" The dreams of sanguine, hopeful youth,
    Are chiefly dreams alone,
Whose falseness often breaks the heart,
    Or turns it into stone.
Fame's or ambition's giddy height
    Is only seldom gain'd,
And often half the pleasure leaves,
    Just when the height's attain'd.

" But still I strive, and still I hope,
    And still I fight the battle,
Besieg'd by earth's artillery,
    With all its horrid rattle.
Then come, ye mocking earthly foes,
    E'en come like fiends of hell,
I'll fight the battle till I die,
    And I will fight it well.

" I'll change my tactics quickly, tho',
    Fight on a diff'rent line,
And on my waving battle flag,
    I'll mark a diff'rent sign.
Until this present moment, I
    Have fought in single strife,
But I will fight no more alone,
    I'll get myself a wife.

" We'll then fight all who dare oppose,
    E'en should it be her brother,
And when we've vanquish'd all our foes,
    We'll turn and fight each other."

F

ODE TO MAN.

A MAN is not what oft he seems,
  On this terrestrial sphere,
No pow'r to wield, no honor'd place,
  Oft curb his spirit here.

He knows not what within him lies,
  Until his pow'rs be tried,
And when for them some use is found,
  They spring from where they hide,

To startle and to puzzle him,
  Who never knew their force,
Because his unfreed spirit kept
  A low and shackl'd course.

Dishearten'd and despairing, he
  Had often sigh'd alone,
Not thinking that in other ways
  His spirit might have grown.

Not thinking that another course,
  Which needed pluck and vim,
Might raise his drowning spirit high,
  And teach it how to swim;

To battle with the rolling tide,
  That hurries onward men,
And raise his head above the waves,
  That come and go again.

A SWAIN TO HIS SWEETHEART.

What subtle charm is in thy voice,
That ever, when I hear its tone,
My heart doth pleasantly rejoice,
And fondly turns to thee alone ?

The mem'ries of a toilsome life
Are banish'd by its potent spell,
And earthly care, and earthly strife,
No whisper'd sorrows dare to tell.

Where hope had fled, new hope inspires;
Comes life, where lately life had gone ;
New purposes my bosom fires,
To battle hard and bravely on.

What charm dwells in thine eye of blue,
That thus; by its magnetic pow'r,
The world to me hath brighter hue,
And happier grows each passing hour ?

With virtuous thought, and pure desire,
Thine eyes look forth from lofty soul ;
Contagious, then, my thoughts aspire
To reach, with thee, thy lofty goal.

Thine eyes contemptuously look down
On all that's sordid, mean and low ;
Around thy head is virtue's crown,
About thy feet is virtue's snow.

THANKSGIVING·DAY.

GOD of the harvest, once again
   Our joyful tones we raise,
For all Thy goodness, day by day,
   We give Thee thankful praise.

With blessings rich, from fertile field,
   And gifts from fruitful tree,
We wish, this day, our thanks to yield
   With earnest hearts, to Thee.

We plough'd the ground, we sow'd the seed,
   But Thou didst send the rain
In grateful show'rs, in time of need,
   And now we've reap'd the grain.

The sun with grateful heat did shine;
   The dew did nightly fall;
And now, for loaded tree and vine—
   We give Thee thanks for all.

The bee, in well-fill'd honey cells,
   Her sweets for us hath stow'd,
The crystal water in the wells,
   For us from springs hath flow'd.

The lowing herd, the prancing steed
   Receiv'd we from Thy hand,
And we, this day, return our meed
   Of praise, throughout the land.

Then let us sing with earnest hearts,
   Tho' joyful be each lay,
And thankful ev'ry song that starts
   On this Thansgiving Day.

A SUNSET.

"OH come," said I unto my love,
  "And let us view the setting sun,
And watch the fleeting clouds above,
  So brightly color'd, ev'ry one."

Thus lightly to my love, I spake,
  And she responded lightly, too,
And by my side her place did take,
  Her young heart gladden'd by the view.

I walk'd along, she tripp'd beside,
  Short was the time, until we stood
Above the rolling, glassy tide—
  Above old Huron's mighty flood.

"Oh, see," said I, " the glorious sight,
  Now spread before our favor'd gaze—
The clouds all flame, the sea all light,
  The sun, one grand, terrific, blaze."

E'en such a time, and such a scene
  Could not love's gentle pow'r dispel.
I saw my love's grave, thoughtful mien,
  I turn'd and said: " your thoughts pray tell."

"My thoughts! Oh yes, since you request,
  My thoughts were centr'd all in you,
As chang'd my gaze from crest to crest,
  Across the glassy ocean's blue ;

"And, as I saw the waters shine
  With polish'd splendor from the sun,
Thus gleam'd, I thought, this love of mine,
  Thus shall it gleam till life is done.

" And, as I saw the bars of gold,
     And clouds with crimson deeply dy'd,
Your love, I thought, was wealth untold,
     And my heart's blood, your crimson tide."

" And yours," I said, " your love to me
     Is one great, shining, glassy flood ;
Your face, reflected, there I see,
     So beautiful, so bright and good.

" My nature glows at thy dear name,
     With deep, red heat, like yonder ball,
It shines with constant, ruddy flame ;
     It shines for you, but tinges all.

" But see, the sun has sunk to rest,
     As if beneath the distant wave,
But still the colors in the west,
     Show that he still shines from his grave.

" And thus, my love, when I shall sink
     Into the dark and dread Unknown,
'Tis surely just for us to think,
     Some rays shall shine for thee alone.

" And if it be my fate to stay,
     While thou shalt calmly sink to rest,
'Tis surely right for me to say,
     Some light from thee shall cheer my breast."

THE MAPLE TREE.

WHERE craggy hills round Madoc rise,
  With scenic grandeur bold,
Where frowning rocks, from wooded heights,
  Look down so stern and cold,

On peaceful vales, and silent lakes,
  And islets, wild and fair,
Where trees, in fadeless beauty clad,
  Display their verdure there.

Where men, undaunted by the force
  Of nature's stern array,
Determin'd, drive a prosp'rous course,
  And honorable way.

Here doth the oak rear high its form,
  The spreading beech beside,
And here the hemlock meets the storm,
  With branches stretching wide.

The pine, with straight and lofty stem,
  The birch, whose shapen rind
Sails o'er the lakes by dusky hands,
  Or favorable wind.

Such trees as those, are widely known,
  And many more beside,
And may be found from Madoc's hills,
  To Huron's waters wide.

Right dear they are to sturdy hearts;
  To pioneers, their name
Lights up the thoughts of other days,
  With bright and cheerful flame.

But dearer far than all of these,
 Than all from sea to sea,
To Canada's brave sons of toil,
 Is the stout maple tree.

The maple tree ! the maple tree !
 Because its leaf so fair,
Is emblem of our Canada,
 And all our hopes are there.

Our country thrives, and so shall we,
 On this, our native sod,
If we respect our maple tree,
 And worship only God.

The maple leaf ! the maple leaf !
 Tho' in the fall it fade,
May it but die, to bloom again,
 And brighten up the glade.

Oh, deeper strike each year thy roots,
 Young Canada's fair tree,
That no rude hand may tear thee up,
 Thou emblem of the free.

If on thy branch an eagle bold,
 Or other bird of prey,
Shall dare with haughtiness to sit,
 May it soon fly away.

GODERICH.

WHERE once the red deer, wolf or bear,
Pursued by hardy Indian braves,
Lay low, in cunning grove or lair,
And listen'd to the rolling waves.

Where once the maple and the beech,
In nature's splendor tower'd high,
Far, far beyond the white man's reach,
Was this lone spot, in years gone by.

The lofty bank, and level plain,
With wide-mouth'd maitland stretch'd to view,
Look'd out upon the inland main,
And back, where virgin forests grew.

No harbor then, nor water-break,
Made by the mind and hand of man,
But fast into the rolling lake,
In nature's course, the river ran.

No pennon stream'd from lofty mast,
No ships were there, propell'd by steam,
For then, instead of whistle blast,
Was heard the lordly eagle's scream.

The light canoe of birchen rind,
Sent o'er the waves by skilful oar,
Express'd so plain the untrain'd mind—
Content with this, it wish'd no more.

No chimneys, tall and massive made,
Show'd where the white man ground his corn,
For there no white man yet had stray'd,
Where but the forest child was born.

And now, where spacious mansions stand,
Where grace and culture now reside,
There clasp'd the Indian brave the hand
Of his own war-won forest bride.

Where once the painted warrior wrote
His thoughts in rudely pictur'd signs,
A cultur'd language now we quote,
And write and print, in graceful lines.

Where once the hieroglyphic bark
Told when the warlike bow should twang,
The torch of light with glowing spark,
Is held aloft by faithful Strang.

But there is yet another flame,
With pure and holy light to shed;
And all revere that honor'd name,
And all respect that rev'rend head.

That hoary head, which, from the place
Where mild religion's beams doth play,
Hath warn'd, implor'd our fallen race,
And pray'd, while years have pass'd away.

Beneficent and kind old man,
Accept our humble tributes now,
And when is run thine earthly span,
May fadeless wreathes entwine thy brow.

VERSES WRITTEN IN AUTOGRAPH ALBUMS.

TO MISS———

YOUTH is the time when all is bright;
　The mind is free from care;
No thoughts of aught, save present joys,
　Can find an entrance there.

And, if a thought of future years
　Steal o'er the careless mind,
That thought speaks of a happier time
　When years are left behind.

But when the years of youth have fled,
. And life is fill'd with pain,
We think full oft of vanish'd years,
　And wish them back again.

And oft this wish will soothe our pain,
　And oft allay our woe,
Oh, sweet to us is mem'ry then,
　When we think of long ago.

May thou live on till youth has pass'd,
　And feel but little pain,
And may thou, in a blest old age,
　Live o'er your youth again.

TO A FRIEND.

WITH kindly thoughts full oft we've met,
And bow'd at Friendship's sacred shrine;
Oh, may we ne'er those thoughts forget,
But may they still our hearts entwine.

May both retain those feelings long,
Which prompt the words of friendly tongue,
May I not fail to think of thee,
Nor you to think of T. F. Young.

To Miss ———

My friend of days, but not of years,
With kindly heart these lines I trace,
To tell you of a kindly wish,
Which I upon this page would place.

It is that thou thro' future years
May meet with very much of joy,
And just a little grief, because
Continued happiness will cloy.

And when, in future years, you read
What I to you just now have sung,
Let others praise or blame, do thou
Think pleasantly of T. F. Young.

To ———

These lines, which on this leaf I write,
I trace with friendly thoughts of thee,
And hope, when o'er this page you glance,
You'll think a kindly thought of me.

And why should I this tribute ask ?
Why crave from you this humble boon ?
Because I knew you through life's morn,
And hope to know you in its noon.

Because the path of life we trod,
With youthful hearts so free from pain,
When both together went to school,
And wander'd gaily home again.

This, then, is why I ask of you,
As on this little page you look,
To think of me, with other friends,
Whose names are witten in your book.

To a Friend.

In years to come, when looking o'er
  These lines I've penn'd for thee,
I trust that thou shalt ne'er have cause
  To think unkind of me.

And if you have, let memory
  Try hard to blunt the dart,
And tho' I may deserve the blame,
  Let kindness soothe the smart.

To a Friend.

The youthful joys of vanish'd years,
  The joys e'en now we share,
Have something of a sacred bliss,
  Which time can not impair.

For when the years of youth have gone,
  Its joys and hopes have flown,
The mem'ry clings with fond embrace—
  Those joys are still our own.

Then, as I write these words for you,—
  This earnest wish I pen :
That you may think but pleasant thoughts—
  When life's liv'd o'er again.

May nought of sorrow, or of woe,
  Invade to wound or pain,
And may the joys that we have shar'd
  Be bright in mem'ry's train.

To Miss ——— .

In tracing here these lines, my friend,
　Which spring from friendly heart,
I here record an earnest wish,
　For thee, before we part :

May health and happiness serene,
　Long, long with thee abide,
May youthful joys no sorrow bring,
　Nor future woes betide.

And when thy youthful beauty leaves,
　And youthful thoughts thy breast,
May thou in calm old age still live,
　 * In happiness and rest.

To a Little Girl.

Go, little girl, your course pursue,
　On life's rough ocean safely glide,
May want nor woe e'er visit you,
　Nor any other ills betide.

Improve the shining hours of youth,
　For soon, alas, they will be gone,
Strive hard for learning, zeal and truth,
　For ev'ry soul must fight alone.

To a Friend.

Within this little book of thine,
　Are thoughts of many a friendly mind,
Express'd in words, on which you'll gaze
　In after years, with feelings kind.

And while you're scanning o'er each page,
   These lines I write, perchance you'll see,
And tho' they're penn'd by careless hand,
   You'll know that they are penn'd by me.

Perhaps you'll think of school-days then,
   Of happy school-days, long since past,
When you and I, in careless youth,
   Thought that those days would always last.

To Master George Twiddy.

G o on your way, my youthful friend,
E arth's joys and woes to feel,
O 'er rough and smooth, your course will tend,
R ight on, thro' woe and weal,
G ird up yourself then, for the fight,
E ach foe to meet without affright.

T hink not too much of joy or woe,
W hich one and all must meet,
I n duty's path still onward go,
D ark days and bright to greet,
D etermin'd still to do your best,
Y our work, be sure, will then be blest.

To Miss ———

T HE fairest flowers often fade,
   And die, alas! too soon,
Ere half their life is sped, they droop,
   And wither in their bloom.

But may thy life thro' future years,
   In healthful beauty shine,
And when you think of other days,
   Think of this wish of mine.

To Miss Milly Scott.

MEMORIES of happy school-days,
In which we view the years gone by,
Long they last, and long they cheer us—
Live well the moments as they fly,
Your youth is passing swiftly by.

See, then, Milly, that your school-days
Can no mem'ries sad retain.
Onward! upward! be your motto,
Try and try, and try again,
The future will reward the pain.

THOMAS MOORE.

THE land of poetry and-mirth,
Of orators and statesmen, too,
To one more genial, ne'er gave birth,
Than when, gay Moore, it brought forth you.

The land of Goldsmith, Wolfe and Burke,
May well, with gladness, sound thy name,
And honor thee, whose life and work
Produc'd a bright and joyous flame.

Thy lively genius, sparkling, free,
Emitted rays, which sparkle yet,
And gladden hearts across the sea,
When tears of pain their eyelids wet.

Mild Goldsmith sang with taste, and well,
And so did Wolfe, his plaintive ode,
But thou, alone, possess'd the spell,
That serv'd to ease thy country's load.

O'Connell work'd with wondrous skill,
With silv'ry tongue, and prudent head,
With patriotic heart and will,
To ease Oppression's crushing tread.

He did remove th' oppressor's weight,
Or made it rest more lightly there,
But still there crowded in the gate
The ills of life we all must share.

Great Burke, with comprehensive mind,
Pour'd forth his thoughts, too lofty far,
To glad his humble, simple kind,
Who could not reach the lowest bar.

But thou brought forth thy tuneful lyre,
And swept it with a skilful hand,
And hearts, with joy and hope afire,
Arose to bless thee, thro' the land.

Thy songs of love, religion, fame,
Resounded from each hill and dale,
And fann'd the patriotic flame,
In beautiful Avoca's vale.

They reach'd us here, we have them now,
And treasure them, both rich and poor;
And here's a green wreath for thy brow,
Of Irish shamrocks, Thomas Moore.

In fadeless verdure may it stay,
And long thy gifted head entwine,
For time will mark full many a day,
Till head and heart shall live, like thine.

———

G

ROBERT BURNS.

ONE hundred years have come and gone,
Since thy brave spirit came to earth,
Since Scotland saw thy genius dawn,
And had the joy to give thee birth.

There was no proud and brilliant throng,
To celebrate thine advent here,
And but the humble heard the song,
Which first proclaim'd a poet near.

But genius will assert its right
To speak a word, or chant a lay,
And thou, with independent might,
Asserted it from day to day.

No fawning, sycophantic whine,
Marr'd the clear note thy spirit blew,
Thy stirring words, thy gift divine,
Were to thyself and country true.

Tho' heir to naught of wealth, or land,
Thy soaring mind, with fancy fir'd,
Saw, in Creation's lavish hand,
The gifts display'd, thy soul desir'd.

The field, the forest and the hill
Supplied thee with exhaustless wealth,
The singing birds, and flowing rill,
Unto thy soul gave food and health.

An honest man thou lov'd, and thou
Wert honest to thy bosom's core,
As harden'd hand, and sweated brow,
A true, tho' silent witness bore.

No empty theorizer, thou,
Thy words said what thyself would do,
Thou ne'er would make thy spirit bow,
That wordly honors might accrue.

Torn by temptations, strange and wild—
Hard-hearted critics laugh to scorn
The fate of the " poetic child,"
In rugged, bonnie Scotland born.

But let them laugh, they laugh in vain,
For they, or we, who know in part,
Can never gauge the mighty strain,
That burst the genial poet's heart.

It is enough for us to know
The songs he sang for Scotland's sake,
Which winds of time can never blow
Into oblivion's silent lake.

O Burns ! thy life was sad, we know,
Thy sensitive and fertile mind
Had to withstand full many a blow,
Dealt by the ignorant and blind.

But let us do thee justice here,
Tho' distant from thy native shore,
For all thy faults repress the sneer,
And thy great qualities explore.

In Canada, where all are free,
And none can e'er be call'd a slave,
Let Scotia's sons remember thee,
And weave a garland for thy grave.

In fancy, let them grace thy brows
With wreathes of fadeless asphodel,
And let them yearly plight their vows
Unto the bard they love so well.

BYRON.

WHILE genius endows the sons of men
With eloquence, or with poetic pen,
It leaves them still the frailties of our frame,
It does not curb, but fans th' unrighteous flame.
It gives a wider, nobler range of thought,
But such advantage, oft, is dearly bought.
Man's lower nature troubles scarce the low,
But, like a fiend, at natures high doth go.
Of such a nature, now, these lines shall tell,
Who wrote full many a line, and wrote them well.
Byron, the noble, sensitive and high,
Whose bosom hath not heav'd for thee a sigh?
Whose breast hath not full often given room
To mournful thoughts, for thy untimely doom?
Thy genius soar'd to regions bright and fair,
And thou, such times, were with thy genius there.
And then thy lofty mind, 'neath passion's sway,
Left its high throne, and wander'd far astray.
'Twas strange and sad, that one so richly bless'd,
Should find within the world, so much unrest;
But we can in thy life and nature see
The means, to some extent, that fell'd the tree.
Thy shining youth, men much too freely prais'd,
And then the cry of blame, too loudly rais'd.
The fickle crowd, thy person loudly curs'd,
And then thou fled, and dar'd them do their worst.
Unfortunate in love, thy youthful heart
Was pain'd, and likewise with the burning smart
Thy vanity receiv'd from critic's pen,
Which often makes sarcastic, stronger men.
Let us be fair with thee, thy fate deplore,
And grieve thy youthful death, if nothing more.
Let us in mercy judge, for thus we can.
E'en with thy faults, thou wert a noble man.

MEMORIES OF SCHOOL DAYS.

THERE are mem'ries glad of the old school-house,
    Which throng around me still;
And voices spoke in my youthful days,
    My ears with music fill.

Those youthful voices I seem to hear,
    With their gladsome, joyous tone,
And joy and hope they bring to me,
    When I am all alone.

I think of the joys of that time long past,
    Of its boyish hopes and fears,
And 'tis partly joy, and partly pain,
    That wets my eyes with tears.

For 'tis joy I feel, when I seem to stand,
    Where I stood long years ago,
And when I think that cannot be,
    My heart is fill'd with woe.

My old school mates are scatter'd far,
    And some are with the dead,
And my old class mates have wander'd, too,
    To seek for fame, or bread.

And those who still are near my home,
    And whom I often see,
Have come to manhood's grave estate;
    They're boys no more to me.

And tho' we meet in converse yet,
    And each one's thoughts enjoy,
Our thoughts and words are not so free,
    As when each was a boy.

For the spring of life is gone for us,
  With all its bursting bloom,
And manhood's thoughts, and joys, and cares,
  Are now within its room.

But the mem'ry of our bright school days,
  Will last through ev'ry strain,
And time will brighten ev'ry joy,
  And darken ev'ry pain.

The rippling of our childhood's laugh,
  Will roll adown the years,
And time will blunt, each day we live,
  The mem'ry of our tears.

Our boyhood's hopes, and boyhood's dreams,
  And aspirations high,
Will doubtless never be fulfill'd,
  Until the day we die.

But still we'll cherish in our hearts,
  And live those days again,
When awkardly we read our books,
  Or trembling held the pen.

SUNRISE.

How few there are who know the pure delight,
  The chaste influence, and the solace sweet,
Of walking forth to see the glorious sight,
  When nature rises, with respect, to greet
The lord of day on his majestic seat,
  Like some great personage of high degree,
Who cometh forth his subjects all to meet,
  Like him, but yet more glorious far than he,
  He comes with splendor bright, to shed o'er land and sea.

With stately, slow and solemn march he comes,
  And gradually pours forth his brilliant rays,
Unheralded by sounding brass or drums,
  His blazing glory on our planet plays,
And sendeth healing light thro' darken'd ways.
  His undimm'd splendor maketh mortals quail,
And e'en, at times, it fiercely strikes and slays;
  But then it brighteneth the cheek so pale,
  Revives the plant, and loosens every nail
  That fastens sorrow to the heart, within this vale.

But 'tis the morning glory of the sun,
  I would request you now to view with me,
'Twill cheer that smitten heart, thou grievéd one,
  And lighter make your load of misery,
  When you can hear and see all nature's glee.
Come friend arise, determin'd, drowse no more,
  But stroll away to yonder hill with me;
And all the landscape round we shall explore,
All nature slumbers now ; its sleep will soon be o'er.

The stillness now is strange, oppressive, grand,
  The hush of death is now o'er all the earth,
As if it slept by power of genius's hand,
  But soon the spell shall break, and songs and mirth,
  And light, shall all proclaim the morning's birth.
E'en now behold the sun's advancing gleams,
  The heralds of his coming, but the dearth
Of words forbid my telling how the streams,
And dewy grass are glinting, sparkling in the beams.

Or of the change, so steady and so sure,
  That creeps upon creation all around,
Unwaken'd yet from slumbers bright and pure,
  By atmospheric change, or earthly sound,
  Such as at times awakes with sudden bound.

There comes a change o'er earth, and trees, and sky,
　　And all creation's work wherever found,
Save man, for he, with unawaken'd eye,
In dozing, slothful ease, will yet for hours lie.

The grandest artificial sights will pall
　　Upon the taste, and oft repeated, tire,
But each succeeding morn, the monarch Sol
　　Bedecks the world with fresh and vig'rous fire,
That cheers the fainting heart and sootheth ire.
　　Each morn, the gazer seeth something new,
And even what he saw will never tire,
　　For in an aspect clear and fresh, the view
Will gladden still your eyes, tho' oft it's gladden'd you.

By slow degrees the heralds make their way,
　　Until, at last, old Sol himself appears,
To reign supreme thro' all ·the blessed day,
　　As he hath reigh'd for many thousand years
　　O'er joy and woe, bright smiles and bitter tears.
The very air is now astir with life,
　　And all around, unto our eyes and ears
Come evidences of a kindly strife,
For fields, and air, and trees with bustling now are rife.

All animated nature seems to vie
　　Each with the other, in their energy
Of preparation for the day's supply
　　Of work or play, or whate'er else may be
　　Prompted for them to do instinctively.
The grass is fill'd with buzzing insect throngs,
　　There's music in the air, and every tree
Is vocal with the wild-bird's gladsome songs,
Songs unrestrain'd by care or memory of wrongs.

A million tiny drops of crystal dew,
  In shining splendor make the meadows fair ;
The leaves upon the trees are greener, too,
  As, swaying in the gentle morning air,
  They are again prepar'd to stand the glare
Of Sol's meridian heat, and give their shade
  To myriads of feather'd songsters there.
Our trip to see the sun arise is made,
  Let us retrace our steps, and bravely share
  Our portion of life's grief, anxiety and care.

LINES IN MEMORY OF THE LATE VEN. ARCH-DEACON ELWOOD, A.M.

WHEN men of gentle lives depart,
They leave behind no brilliant story
Of fam'd exploits, to make men start
In wonder at their dazzling glory.

The scholar's light, religion's beams,
Tho' fill'd with great, commanding pow'r,
In modest greatness throw their gleams,
In quiet rays, from hour to hour.

The greatest battles oft are fought,
Unseen by any earthly eye ;
The victors all alone have wrought,
And, unapplauded, live or die.

'Twas thus with thee, thou rev'rend man ;
In peaceful, holy work thy life
Was spent, until th' allotted span
Was cut by Time's relentless knife.

II

Far from the keen and heartless train,
Who daily feel Ambition's sting,
Thy life, remov'd, felt not the pain,
Which goads each one beneath her wing.

What pains thou felt, what joys thou knew,
Who shall presume to think or tell ?
But this we know : there daily grew
Within thy heart, a living well.

That well of love increas'd each day,
The milk of human kindness flow'd,
And cheer'd the faint ones on their way,
Along a hard and toilsome road.

Thy voice rang out for years and years,
In fancy, yet, we hear its roll,
And see thy face, thro' blinding tears,
Fill'd with a love for ev'ry soul.

Thy words we shall not soon forget,
Thy deeds shall be remember'd, too,
And now, while ev'ry eye is wet,
Let us accord thee honor due.

Thou battl'd not 'gainst hosts of hell,
With words alone, convincing, warm ;
Thy deeds were like the fatal shell,
That bursts amid the battle's storm.

The temple now, which stately stands
A lasting monument, shall tell
Of lib'ral hearts, and willing hands,
Urg'd on by thee to labor well.

O father, friend, we'll see no more !
Thy fight is done, and it was long ;
But thou hast reach'd another shore,
And singeth now a blessed song.

The snows shall come upon the hills,
The valleys, too, with white be spread,
The birds shall whistle by the rills,
The flowers shall their fragrance shed.

The spring shall come to deck the earth,
In garb of vernal loveliness;
And sorrow shall abound, and mirth
Betimes shall cheer our deep distress.

The seasons shall perform their rounds,
And vegetation bloom and fade,
But thou wilt heed nor sights nor sounds,
For thou to rest for aye art laid.

ST. PATRICK'S DAY.

THE chilly days of March are here,
The raw, cold winds are blowing;
All nature now, is bleak and drear,
But piercing winds and frosts are going.

But frosts nor snows, nor biting blast,
Can chill the warmth within each heart,
When comes around the day at last,
To sainted mem'ry set apart.

For many centuries thy name,
St. Patrick, has been warmly bless'd,
And many more thy righteous fame
Shall animate each Christian breast.

Each Christian, and each patriot, too,
Shall celebrate for years, the day,
And show the world that they are true
To virtuous worth, long pass'd away.

Oh, Ireland! for many years
Unhappy thou hast been, and sore,
But long, we're thankful thro' our tears,
Sweet songs have sounded from thy shore.

While other lands in bitter strife
Fought wildly for kingship or gold,
The words of peace, the way of life,
Within fair Ireland were told.

The Druid priests their rites forbore,
And listen'd to the words that fell
From Patrick's pious lips, as o'er
The land he told his story well.

His lips told of the way of life;
His self-denying actions, too,
Enforc'd the truth, where all was rife
With wrongful rites of darken'd hue.

The people listen'd to his voice,
And learn'd to love the faith he taught;
When fruits arose in after years,
They bless'd the name of him who wrought.

Who wrought successfully to place
Religion's light within the land—
A benefit to all his race,
At home, or on a foreign strand.

Religion's light shone clear and bright,
And then the lesser lights appear'd;
Learning arose with quiet might,
And simple minds it rais'd and cheer'd.

Old Tara's heathen temple rung
With sounds, whose waves are rolling yet,
From which unmeasur'd good has sprung,
Which grateful hearts will not forget.

The triple leaf—St. Patrick's flow'r—
Long may it grow, long may it bear
Those symbols of the mighty Pow'r,
That rules the sea, the earth, the air.

The Shamrock ! may our hearts entwine,
And meet in one, as it, tho' three ;
And may your patron Saint, and mine,
Our patron saint forever be.

THE END.

www.ingramcontent.com/pod-product-compliance
Lightning Source LLC
Chambersburg PA
CBHW022140020726
47496CB00008B/2482